ARTHUR BLACKWOOD'S
SCARY STORIES
FOR KIDS WHO LIKE SCARY STORIES
BOOK #1

A.M. LUZZADER

For Cohen
I hope this book scares you, but not too much

CHAPTER 1
YOUR INTRODUCTION TO ARTHUR BLACKWOOD

HELLO. Welcome. Please come in.

I'm so glad you're here, but dear me, you're soaked to the skin! Let me take that coat from you. Oh, it's drenched! The thunderstorm is still raging, eh? Yes, look at it out there—the wind and rain has been beating on the window panes all evening like some wild night-beast. Well, never mind. We'll go into the study, where it's warm. I'll hang your coat by the fire to dry, and I'll make us something hot to drink.

Come, come. This way.

You know, I was thinking that *I* know who *you* are, and *you* know who *I* am, but we've never actually met, have we? We should officially introduce ourselves.

I am Arthur Blackwood, and as you know, I am a collector of scary stories, terrifying tales, and frightening fantasies.

I am most pleased to finally meet you in person. Come along. Up the stairs. We're nearly there. It's just through here.

Now, I'm told that you are also interested in tales of the horrifying and weird. Is that why you've come all this way? I'm aware that my home is not easy to find, here on this lonely, wooded hill, at the end of that narrow, muddy little trail. And I'm sure this storm was of no help. In any case, am I to understand that you've come all this way to hear a few stories?

Very well. Yes, I'd be happy to oblige.

And here we are—my study, my haunted library, my storytelling chamber. Come in. Won't you have a seat? Here, take this chair, closest to the fireplace. I'll sit in the other.

Please watch your step, however. Yes, I hadn't noticed that it got quite dark while I was waiting for you. My apologies. Let me build up this fire and light a candle.

There, that's a bit brighter, isn't it?

And warmer, too. I'll hang your coat here, and let's set this kettle of cider near the fire to warm up.

Are you drying out yet? There are blankets in the basket there at your feet. Do make yourself at home.

Yes, I would turn on the lights, but I have found that a fire in a fireplace is best for telling stories. Especially on a night like tonight, with the sky so dark and the weather so monstrous. Candle light works, too, or flashlights in a pinch. There's more to storytelling than just words, you know. A good story requires a certain setting, especially when it comes to stories of the darker sort.

For example, see there—that suit of armor standing there in the corner. Didn't notice it before, did you? Yes, it's made of black iron and doesn't really stand out when the light is low this way. However, now that you see it in the flickering gloom, does it not seem to be alive? To breathe? As though there were someone inside it, waiting? A phantom from a lost age, perhaps. Would you like to go over there and look into the visor?

What about that crystal ball on the mantle? There, next to the candlestick. Interesting the way it seems to glow with its own weird light, don't you think? Surely, it's full of dark, brooding magic. What secrets might it tell us if we were to gaze into it? What does the future hold for you? Is it fortune? Or doom?

Now take a look at that stuffed tarantula on the end table. Yes, just there by your elbow. Huge, isn't it? You hadn't seen that, either, had you? Well, now you'll notice how the firelight glistens upon its fangs and bristles, and how the eight eyes—beads of black glass—reflect tiny points of flame. Also see how the flicker of the fire makes the giant spider appear to emerge from the shadows and creep in your direction, as though it were very much alive and ready to mindlessly sink its fangs into your wrist.

Consider what would happen if you carelessly flipped on a lamp. Or what if I turned on all the lights, even only for a brief moment? The sinister suit of armor would transform into just another dusty artifact, the magic would drain from the crystal ball like water from a leaky pail, and you'd see that the tarantula is lifeless and stuffed with harmless fluff.

However, with the darkness pressing in from that endless dark forest outside, and with only firelight to see by, it's entirely different. The tarantula is alive and deadly, the crystal ball can tell strange secrets, and the armor is haunted.

Anything is possible in the dark!

And that is what we need if we are going to tell scary stories—we must have endless possibilities all around us at all times. Don't you agree? I thought you would. It's settled then—we'll keep the lights off for now.

Before we begin, I must inquire if you frighten easily? Are you easily scared? I only ask because I saw your eyes grow a bit wider when you noticed the suit of armor, and you might have flinched a little when I pointed out the stuffed spider on the end table.

A word of caution: my stories are not for the faint-hearted. They are not to be taken lightly. I'd hate to hand you a bigger shock than you were expecting, especially at an hour as late and dark as this one.

I see.

So you actually enjoy being frightened, do you? Excellent. I think we'll get along very well. Ah, see, the cider is warm now. Help yourself.

Are these stories true? You raise a very good question, one that I am often asked. However, I must inform you that your question is not terribly meaningful. You see, all stories are true in one way or another, especially those meant to frighten, those meant to disturb.

As I told you already, with the storm howling over our heads, and the darkness lurking around us, anything is possible.

CHAPTER 2
RABBIT'S PARK

Finn Finnegan and his younger sister, Durvla, were nasty and unpleasant little children.

I'm sorry, but there's no better way to say it.

Yes, the Finnegan kids were rotten, but those who are rotten often get what's coming to them in the most ghastly ways.

Finn and Durvla lived with their parents in a tall row house on East 5th Street in South Boston. Finn was twelve years old. He stood tall with broad shoulders and a big, round, angry face.

Durvla was ten. She was short and wispy. On her face she wore a permanently sly expression, and she crept from place to place like a ghost.

Don't let the difference in their ages fool you—little Durvla was as obnoxious as her rather gigantic brother, and maybe more so. No one knew why they were so beastly, but even at such tender ages, Finn and Durvla had already racked up an impressive list of misdeeds.

Do you remember when someone doorbell-ditched every single door along all of K Street? The Finnegan siblings did that. Please don't ask how I know. Frail old men and ladies with walkers, busy mothers with bawling babies, people whose cats darted out of any open door—Finn and Durvla forced them all to answer their doors for no good reason. The two rascals first progressed from north to south, hid out for a while, then doorbell-ditched the whole street again from south to north.

A remarkable feat of endurance, I admit, but very mean-spirited.

Did you hear about the vandalism at St. Augustine's church on Dorchester Street? Again, don't ask how I know, but *that* was the Finnegans, too. The two attended church at St. Augustine's (when their parents could make them go, that is), and they knew where every church member preferred to sit. And so, beneath the cloak of darkness, Finn and Durvla broke into the church one Saturday night and, using flashlights and heavy black crayons, scrawled rude insults all over the benches.

On the bench where the McMurdy family always sat, Finn wrote, *Meet the McMurdys, who are all dumb and dirty*. On the Widow Ryan's bench, Durvla wrote, *Old Mrs. Ryan is always cryin'*. This was quite a shocking thing to see on a Sunday morning, I assure you. I won't repeat what they scribbled about poor Mr. and Mrs. McCarter, but you can probably guess.

And it *was* clever to come up with 185 different naughty taunts, I admit, but it was scandalous nonetheless.

Finn and Durvla were not only scallywags, they were bullies, too. They bullied their enemies, classmates, family members, friends, and even each other.

Finn handled the rough stuff. His specialty was bonking kids on the head with his own English grammar textbook, which he never once opened. But he also enjoyed kicking, punching, and shoving.

Durvla did all the sneaky bullying. She specialized in tripping. Tiny little Durvla could trip a full-grown sixth-grader into a mud puddle and then vanish entirely. In the lunchroom, she was known to trip three kids simultaneously, sending food trays flying in all directions—while the Jell-O on her own tray barely jiggled.

Bullies usually like to focus their aggression on

one special victim, and Durvla and Finn's favorite was a fourth-grader named Bridget O'Hare. Bridget was a nice little girl. Her hair was red and she wore eyeglasses with thick black plastic frames. Why had the Finnegans decided to torment Bridget? Who can say? Perhaps it was because Bridget's nose was always in a book (bullies don't care for those who read a lot). Or maybe it was because Bridget had lots of friends and almost always wore a faint smile (bullies can't stand anyone who seems happier than themselves). Personally, I think it's because Finn and Durvla knew deep down that there was something special about Bridget O'Hare, something powerful.

One day, Bridget sat on a swing in her favorite little South Boston park. (South Boston was known for its many parks.) Some were spacious, like Moakley Park, where all the baseball diamonds were. There were also tiny parks that covered less than one square block. There were parks for young kids, old kids, joggers, bikers, hikers, and there were many parks just for dogs.

Bridget was fond of Sweeney Park on West 5th Street, which boasted a nice jungle gym and basketball hoops, and she often played in Buckley Park up on 3rd Street because it had brand-new playground equipment. But Bridget's favorite was Sunflower

Park. It was small, surrounded by trees, and featured just one old swing-set with only three swings. Most people didn't even know about Sunflower Park, and *that* was why it was Bridget's favorite—it was quiet and usually empty. You see, while Bridget had very nice friends, she often liked being alone.

There was Bridget in Sunflower Park, swinging gently in the middle swing, and reading her book. It was a beautiful autumn day. It had rained a little that morning. Now the sun was out and the trees were showing their finest fall colors.

But Bridget's peaceful solitude was interrupted by a coarse, cruel voice behind her.

"Well, if it ain't Bridget the Booger-Eater!"

It was Finn Finnegan. Bridget assumed Durvla must be sneaking around nearby, too.

You've probably heard that if someone bullies you, you should "just stand up to them." If a bully punches you in the nose, for example, you should punch him right back.

This is poor advice.

First of all, it's a good way to land yourself in trouble, not to mention getting yourself a black eye to go with your bloody nose. Violence just isn't a very good solution to any problem. And in this case,

Bridget wasn't tall enough to even *reach* Finn's nose, let alone punch him there.

A better way to handle bullies is to avoid them if you can and ignore them if you can't. This was Bridget's approach, and she had been very effective lately at avoiding both Durvla and Finn. She'd evaded them for weeks. But Bridget's luck had finally run out, and so now it was time to try ignoring them.

"Hey, you're right," screeched Durvla. "It's Bridget the Booger-Eater!"

Bridget pressed her eyes shut but kept swinging. Maybe they would move on and leave her alone. Oh, but how she hated that awful *nickname*. Finn had come up with it a couple years earlier, when he'd spotted Bridget innocently picking her nose. (You must be aware that *all* children pick their noses no matter how hard they try to deny it.) Bridget hadn't actually *eaten* any boogers, but she did get upset and cry when Finn called her "Bridget the Booger-Eater." That was her downfall—if you let a bully know that something really bothers you, they'll never stop doing that thing to you. Bridget later tried to pretend it *didn't* bother her, but it was too late. The name not only stuck, it evolved into several variations, including "Booger-Muncher," "Boogie-Woogie

Booger-Eater," and the dreaded "Bridget O'Hambooger."

Finn lumbered up to Bridget and stood in front of her like a massive, chubby fortress. Durvla slinked around behind Bridget like an unattached shadow. Finn stopped Bridget's swing from swinging, while Durvla snatched the book from Bridget's hands and tossed it ruthlessly into the nearby shrubbery.

"Sooo," snarled Durvla, showing herself at last, "*thiiis* is where you've been hiding out. Finny! We've found Bridget O'Hambooger's secret hideout!"

"Yeah!" said Finn, holding out the big palm of his beefy hand. "Now gimme your lunch money!"

"I can't give you my lunch money, Finn," grumbled Bridget.

"Why not?" said Finn with an awful scowl.

"Well, for one thing it's 4:30 in the afternoon," Bridget explained. "Lunch is over. And besides, it's *Saturday*."

"Oh yeah," said Finn, blinking stupidly. "Well then, you owe me double next time."

Bridget realized that ignoring her bullies was not working. She'd have to resort to some other strategy.

One of the best anti-bully strategies is to simply report them to a teacher, parent, or some other adult. If you do this, the bully might accuse you of being a "chicken," "rat," "maggot," or some other small and harmless animal. However, it really is one of the best strategies because it will probably be good for the bully, too. Most bullies are deeply unhappy, lonely, and have lots of problems of their own, and adults may often be of great service to them.

Unfortunately, there were no adults available just then. Also, there was one thing Finn and Durvla were right about: there really *was* something special about Bridget. And so she decided to use a different strategy: mind games.

"My *hideout?*" coughed Bridget sarcastically. "You think *this* crummy little park is my hideout? Ha! You'll *never* find my *real* hideout, and even if you do, you'll never *dare* to go there." And with this, Bridget stuck out her tongue, hopped down from the swing, and went to fetch her book from the shrubbery.

Finn gave Bridget a hard shove. Bridget staggered backward and little Durvla tripped her from behind. Bridget fell into a mud puddle.

"Waddya mean by that?" asked Finn. "I ain't afraid of *nothing*."

"Well, *that's* a double-negative," muttered Bridget, "and it actually means that you *are* afraid."

"Enough of your big words, Booger-Muncher!"

cried Durvla. "We know you've been avoiding us. Tell us where your *real* hideout is!"

"I can't!" argued Bridget, getting up from the mud. "It's where my friends hide, too!"

Durvla leaned toward Finn and in a raspy whisper she hissed, "Finny! I've heard Boogie-Woogie-Booger-Eater has *lots* of friends! Think of all that lunch money!"

A wicked grin spread across Finn's face. Bridget was searching the shrubbery for her book. Finn and Durvla advanced on her, slowly, side by side.

"You'll tell us where that hideout is," rasped Durvla, "or my brother will thump your head."

Bridget backed away. "Never!" she said, but her voice quavered.

"Finny," sneered Durvla, "prepare to thump."

Without taking his beady eyes off Bridget, Finn unslung his backpack and with a pale meaty paw, he reached inside. Thumping kids on their heads was the only thing Finn Finnegan ever did with books. He never read or studied them. His English textbook was his favorite weapon. At 405 pages long, it was heavy but not too thick to grip effectively. If Finn was feeling merciful, he might use his math book, which was only 322 pages long and delivered a slightly less-jarring head-thump. Sometimes, when

Finn was actually feeling *nice*, he'd thump you with his health class textbook, which was a practically weightless 210 pages long.

But today, Finn drew out his World History textbook, the biggest book in the backpack. At a whopping 699 pages, it was the bully's head-bonking nuclear bomb.

Bridget's eyes opened wide as she watched the massive volume slide out from the backpack. She took a few steps back, but Durvla had somehow slipped behind her again. Durvla neatly hooked Bridget's ankle, and Bridget fell into the mud once more. Finn took the history textbook in both fists and raised it high over his head.

Bridget held out her hands to fend off the attack, then whimpered, "Okay! I'll tell you where the hideout is. But you really shouldn't go there. Honest!"

Durvla stood over Bridget with her hands on her hips. She narrowed her eyes and said, "Why *not*?"

"It's cursed!" Bridget confessed, her gaze falling first on Finn, then Durvla. "It's hexed! It's full of witchcraft!"

With what was obviously a great deal of mental effort, Finn reasoned, "If it's full of witchcraft, then— how come—*you* can go there?"

Bridget thrust out her chin and smiled a little. She said, "I can go there because, well, because *I'm* a witch."

For a single moment, Finn and Durvla's faces darkened with doubt and worry. Something about the sincere expression in Bridget's deep brown eyes made them pause.

Then they burst out in whoops of laughter.

Interestingly, if either one of them had ever bothered to open *any* halfway-decent history book, they'd know that the entire state of Massachusetts has a rich legacy of witchcraft, hexes, and curses.

"Where's the hideout?" demanded Finn. He was still laughing, but he held the massive history book in one hand, and he thumped it on the palm of the other.

It went, *Whump, whump, whump.*

Bridget gave in at last. Her eyes fell to the ground and in a soft, sad voice she said, "It's— Rabbit's Park."

"Never heard of it," sneered Durvla. "There's no such place."

"It's in Dorchester Heights," said Bridget, pointing in that direction. "Just follow the crooked little side-road between the old graveyard and the abandoned jailhouse. It's not hard to find once you know it's there. In fact, I'm pretty sure most of my friends are playing there right now."

Durvla and Finn traded a skeptical glance, and then they scowled hard at Bridget.

"C'mon, Durv," said Finn. "Let's go check it out." He thumped his palm with the history book and said, "You better not be lyin' to us."

Something else that Durvla and Finn did not know was that Bridget *never* told lies.

"Durvla!" shouted Bridget. "Finn! Don't go! This is your last warning!"

The two hooligans ignored Bridget and wandered off in the direction of Dorchester Heights. Neither one of them even bothered to look back, and so neither saw what happened next. It was the strangest thing, something you'd only see in a place where there was lots of witchcraft. First, when Bridget turned to fetch her book, a small figure emerged from the shrubbery. Believe it or not, it was a jackrabbit. The rabbit handed Bridget her book. Bridget accepted it, patted the rabbit's head, and then the rabbit ran off—also in the direction of Dorchester Heights.

Meanwhile, Finn and Durvla found Rabbit's Park. Bridget had told the truth. It was just where she said it would be.

But night was falling, and a thunderstorm gathered. The two toughies shivered as they walked down the crooked side-road between the graveyard and the abandoned jailhouse. This was a wild area of town, where vacant lots grew weeds and crooked trees. Crumbling old buildings rose into the dark, stormy sky.

"Feels like someone's watchin' me," grumbled Finn, his eyes darting. "Or some*thing*."

"That's j-j-just your imagination," stuttered Durvla, but her voice was so timid, her brother hardly heard her.

Finn and Durvla stood in the middle of Rabbit's Park. It wasn't much. Trees and brushy hedges lined the outer margin. In the middle there grew a field of uncut grass. Autumn leaves blew merrily around Finn and Durvla in little taunting whirlwinds.

"So, she *was* lyin'!" growled Finn. "This place is empty! That little *worm*. I'll give her a good thumping next time we find her."

Durvla pointed across the shaggy grass of the park. "F-F-Finn? Who's that over there?"

Finn looked. It had gotten darker, but on the far side of the park, they saw a small figure standing alone in the grass. It wasn't a child or even a person. It was too small. Finn and Durvla stared at it.

The little figure stared back.

Then another one just like it appeared from the shadows of the hedge. They recognized its hopping motion. They were rabbits, standing on their hind legs. Jackrabbits.

In case you've never seen one, jackrabbits are not small nor cute nor cuddly like domestic bunny rabbits. Jackrabbits are tall and stringy, with red rodent eyes, coarse fur, translucent ears, and large buck teeth.

Finn snorted. "What's those rabbits doin'?"

The two rabbits were quite far away. Farther than Finn could throw a football. But then another rabbit appeared, and then a few more. They all stood silently together. All jackrabbits. More came. Within a few seconds, there were fifty jackrabbits standing side by side on their back legs. They faced Durvla and Finn.

There was a flash of lightning and suddenly the Finnegan siblings realized, no, there were *not* fifty rabbits.

There were hundreds of them. Finn and Durvla were completely surrounded.

As the thunder boomed, Durvla and Finn Finnegan turned round and round, their backs together. The rabbits encircled them, and more were showing up. Soon there were far too many to count, a low wall of rabbits, a wall with no openings.

"What's goin' on here, Finny?" groaned Durvla.

"I dunno, Durv," breathed Finn.

The sun had set, but when the lightning strobed again, the Finnegans saw that the rabbits were closing in on them now, hopping forward one by one and a little at a time. The circle tightened. Soon the jackrabbits were so close that Finn could gaze into their blank red eyes. Durvla saw a sea of twitching ears and wriggling noses. Their big buck-teeth gleamed in the lightning's glare.

"What should we do, Finny?" whined Durvla.

"I dunno, Durv," breathed Finn.

The bullies hugged in the darkness. No light remained, but now they could *hear* faint, hopping footfalls coming ever closer through the grass. They heard the strange quiet whimpering noise rabbits make.

It began to rain.

Finally, the rabbits brushed against the two kids in the darkness with their cold, damp fur. There were so many now, it couldn't be helped. They crowded in. Finn and Durvla couldn't take a step in any direction. Finn cried out and kicked feebly at the unseen rodents. Little Durvla shrieked when she felt what could only be the cold touch of a jackrabbit nose on her cheek.

"Durv," cried Finn, "I'm scared!"

"I thought you said you weren't scared of nothin'," croaked Durvla.

"I did," whimpered Finn.

The rising wind snatched away their final screams, and the Finnegan siblings were never again heard from.

CHAPTER 3
THE BLACK ARMOR

ROBBY DOBALINA DIDN'T WANT to go to the museum. It was the first week of summer vacation, and Robby had planned to spend the day eating junk food and playing video games like "Warriors & Warlocks" and "Vikings & Valor." He wasn't planning to even change out of his pajamas, let alone go outside.

But his mother, Sylvia, said they were taking a family trip to an art museum in Chicago. And so for the past hour, Robby, in his pajamas, had been complaining and pleading.

"I hate museums!" growled Robby.

"You can't hate *all* museums unless you've been to every single one," answered Robby's mother.

"I want to stay *home!*" groaned Robby.

"You want to play video games all day," answered his mother.

"I'll do anything if you let me stay home!" moaned Robby. "I'll do the dishes for a week!"

"You'll do dishes for *two* weeks if you don't stop complaining," his mother answered. "Museums are interesting and educational and inspirational, and we are *going.*"

"I don't want to be in this family anymore!" Robby shouted. Then he stormed out of the house, slammed the door, and sat on the front steps.

"Stupid museums," spat Robby. "Who cares about a bunch of old pictures?"

Robby was twelve years old and had been to only a few museums, none of which were to his liking. The first was the National Gallery. Robby had gone there with his class during a school field trip to Washington, D.C. The place was filled with countless rooms where paintings hung on every wall.

Here's what Robby said about it: "Half of the pictures are weird old people from ancient history, and the rest are just random splotches of paint!"

On a trip to Missouri with his grandparents, Robby had been forced into another museum that displayed nothing but artifacts from the *Titanic*, the famous sunken ship.

Here's what Robby said about that museum: "*Titanic?* More like *Why*-tanic. *Why* stand around looking at some dusty old chair or teacups or a pocket watch that's a hundred years old?"

In truth, Robby's father, Carl, wanted to stay home, too, to mow the lawn and watch baseball on TV. Robby's big sister, Marie, wanted to go swimming with her friends.

But Robby's mother had *insisted*. This was something she did when she absolutely had to have her way. For example, each year she *insisted* that Robby buy Marie a nice birthday present. And she *insisted* that Robby use his best manners whenever they visited their Aunt Fran. Robby's mother insisted only when the occasion was special, but it always worked. It was like a superpower.

She said, "This is one of the finest art museums in the country, it's only one hour away, and we've never been there. I *insist* that we go!"

And just like that, Robby's whole day was ruined.

Marie said, "Okay, Mom. I'm in. I can go swimming tomorrow."

And Carl said, "Yeah, the lawn can wait. This will be fun!"

"Those traitors," Robby muttered to himself. "This family is the *worst!*"

And so they all got into the car. Robby brought his phone, which had a few games on it, such as "Broadswords & Barbarians" and "Druids & Dragons." Robby figured he could play video games during the drive and while his family wandered around the stupid museum. It wouldn't be as fun as playing games at home, but it would be better than no video games at all.

They had gone to Chicago many times before. They'd visited Lake Michigan and they'd seen the "Cloud Gate," an outdoor sculpture that looked like a massive, stainless-steel chili bean.

"I've already *been* to Chicago," Robby muttered as he buckled up, "and it's not that great."

And so Robby played games on his phone for the entire drive. He refused to join in with his parents and sister as they talked and laughed. He wouldn't sing along to songs on the stereo. And he didn't care to watch the scenery change from corn fields and lakes to tall buildings and narrow city streets. He'd gotten through five levels of "Mazes & Minotaurs" when the car stopped.

"Okay, everyone, let's go," said Robby's mother.

"We've only got six hours, and I want to see *everything!*"

Robby groaned and unbuckled his seatbelt.

Outside the museum, there stood two gigantic bronze lions, one at either side of the stairs that led up to the front entrance. These seemed to scowl at Robby as he climbed the steps, as if they knew he didn't want to be there, as if they knew what was about to happen.

The museum was crowded with people. Sylvia made Robby hold her hand so that he wouldn't get lost. Not only did this make it difficult to play with his phone, it was quite humiliating. Robby trudged along behind his mother, complaining all the while. He refused to believe so many people were willing to come to a museum instead of staying home.

Marie, on the other hand, was enjoying herself. She fell in love with the miniatures gallery. It was a series of corridors and windows through which tiny rooms could be seen. They were the kind of rooms you'd find in a dollhouse, but these miniature rooms were created by a miniatures *artist*, and so they were all perfectly detailed and realistic.

"Wow!" cried Marie. "Look at the tiny dinner plates! Oh! And the little piano! And look at this bedroom! They're all so tiny! Wow!"

Robby scoffed and said, "Yeah, the only thing smaller than these miniature rooms is my interest in looking at them."

Carl's favorite moment was when they all went to the snack bar for lunch. He ordered an authentic Chicago hot dog with everything—pickles, onions, hot peppers, olives, tomatoes, sauerkraut, cheese, more onions, a few more hot peppers, and lots of mustard.

"Dad," sneered Robby, "you're gonna get heartburn, and your breath is gonna smell like battery acid all day!"

Robby's mother enjoyed everything. She marveled at every painting and sculpture. She consulted a little booklet with a map of the museum, then dragged Robby to see all the paintings by someone named Monet (pronounced "MOAN-ay"). Next she wanted to see all the paintings by Manet (pronounced "MAN-ay).

"Oh brother," said Robby, tossing his head and rolling his eyes. "I guess we can't go home until we see EEN-ay, MEEN-ay, and MY-nay, too."

"Ooo," breathed his mother each time she came to a new painting. "Aww. Stunning."

"What's really stunning is how *bored* I am," Robby carped.

But then something caught Robby's eye.

It was a flash of steel, the gleam of metal. Sylvia was dragging him along when down a narrow corridor Robby saw a door that opened onto a small room. Robby tugged back on his mother's hand and through the distant door he saw what he thought was a suit of armor.

"Come *on*, Robby," said his mother, tugging him onward like a cat on a leash. "Keep up."

But Robby managed to slow her down for another moment while he strained for a better look. Yes, there was a suit of armor there! Maybe more than one! And before his mother dragged him away, he also saw medieval helmets and weapons hanging on a wall. It looked like something out of the video game "Knights & Knaves." Robby got only a glimpse before his mother wrenched him away, but he knew what he'd seen.

"Mom!" he yelped, trying to escape his mother's grasp. "I want to go back *there!*"

"Where?" asked Sylvia.

"Back there," cried Robby, pointing with his free hand. "There's a room with swords and armor and weapons."

Robby's mother and father turned to see, but there were so many people and doors and passageways, it was impossible to know what Robby was pointing to.

"I don't see any armor or swords," said Robby's father.

Robby's mother looked at her museum booklet. "Hmm," she said. "I don't see it on the map, either. Why not come with us to see the Rembrandt paintings, and then we'll maybe come back later."

"Nooo," whined Robby, yanking his hand away from her. "I want to see the armor! I want to see the swords! Just leave me here and come back for me later."

Sylvia and Carl looked at one another, pleased that Robby had found *something* to be interested in. They shrugged and turned to Robby.

"Okay," said Sylvia sternly. "We'll meet you *right here* when the museum closes, at six o'clock."

Robby agreed, turned, and was soon lost in the crowd.

And he was right. It was a gallery full of medieval armor and weapons. There were suits of chainmail for footmen, rusted Viking helmets, and full sets of polished steel armor for knights. There were spears and pole-axes, swords and war-hammers.

And all of it was real.

It had all been used by real knights and warriors.

At last Robby was away from his family and seeing something that was *actually* interesting. He looked at every exhibit one by one, and he read all of the dates and descriptions.

At the end of the gallery, over into a dark corner, there stood a rather peculiar suit of armor. First of all, it wasn't made of silvery polished steel like most of the others. But neither was it rusted and dull like some of the older exhibits. Instead, this armor was black.

Secondly, it was not as tall as the others. Remarkably, this suit of armor was about Robby's size. And finally, the armor wasn't labeled like the other exhibits. It was encircled with a velvet rope with the usual sign reading DO NOT TOUCH, but it had no description like all the other exhibits had.

And yet, the armor was exquisite. The way the plates fit together and overlapped was amazing. Robby stepped closer. The rivets and fittings were so expertly crafted. There was only the velvet rope between Robby and the suit of armor. He reached out to touch it.

"I wouldn't do that," said a voice.

Robby spun around and saw an old man in a tie and a dark-blue blazer. His head was smooth and bald, but he had a wild gray beard and sharp, piercing eyes. Where had he come from? He wore no name badge, but Robby figured he was one of those museum workers who strolled around telling everyone, "Don't touch. Don't touch. Don't touch." Robby thought this was another boring thing about museums—you couldn't touch anything.

"Don't touch," said the old man.

"Or *what?*" said Robby grumpily. "You'll kick me out? Because I would *love* that. I don't even want to *be* here. My mom made me come."

"You've been warned," said the old man, raising his bushy eyebrows. "Don't touch the exhibits. Especially not *that* one."

Robby turned away to look at the armor. "Why not *this* one?" he asked. "Is it because it's so amazing? Where is it from? Who did it belong to? When was it made? Why doesn't it have a description? It's just my size, you know. If you didn't have stupid rules about not touching anything, I might be able to *wear* this." Robby turned back to the old man.

But he wasn't there.

Robby looked around. The old man was gone. Robby was the only person in the entire gallery. He thought this was slightly odd, but he quickly turned his attention back to the incredible suit of black armor.

He noticed that one reason this suit of armor stood apart from the others was the way it was posed. The other armor suits were hung somewhat awkwardly from wooden frames, almost like coats hanging from racks. Or they were placed on stuffed-cloth dummies that slouched and tilted unnaturally.

But the small suit of black armor stood up on its own, with its armored feet planted firmly on the floor, as if a real person were wearing the armor but standing very still.

Robby stepped closer to the armor, brushing up against the velvet rope.

He examined the helmet. It was a jousting helmet that covered the entire face of the wearer. Only a narrow slot was provided for the knight to see through.

"Wow!" breathed Robby.

What a thrill it would be to wear such a magnificent suit of armor in a jousting tournament during the middle ages! But, Robby thought, it would be awesome enough just to *wear* the suit, even if it were only for a short time.

Robby leaned farther across the velvet rope.

And that's when he saw something. Through the slot in the visor, inside the helmet, he saw a pair of eyes looking back at him. Were they real? Or was it a mannequin? It was dark inside the helmet and diffi-cult to see. Robby looked closer. Yes, there *was* a face within the helmet. At first Robby drew back, startled, but then he looked through the slot again.

"Is someone inside there?" Robby asked softly.

There came no sound, but Robby thought the helmet nodded just a little, as if to say, "Yes," but it was almost too slight to even notice.

Robby gasped. "You're—you're *alive?*"

The helmet nodded again, very slightly.

"Who are you? Can you talk? Can you move?" asked Robby.

Now the helmet moved from side to side, just a little.

"You can't move? Why not?" Robby asked. "Is this your job? You wear the armor and you're not allowed to move?"

The helmet nodded again, only this time it moved enough to make a slight metallic squeaking sound.

"Listen," said Robby. He looked secretively around the gallery. There was still no one else around. Robby lowered his voice and said, "I know this is probably against the rules about touching stuff in the museum, but, do you think I could wear this armor? There's no one here. I won't tell

35

anyone. Only for a minute or two. I just want to try it on."

This time it was quite unmistakable—the armor eagerly nodded, "Yes."

"Okay. What should I do?" asked Robby. "Should I help you take the armor off?"

This time Robby heard a very faint *voice.*

"What was that?" said Robby, turning his ear to the visor. "I didn't hear you."

What Robby heard was less than a whisper. It said, "*Take—my—hand.*"

"Take your *hand? That's it?*"

Another nod and a hiss of breath that might have been a "*Yes.*"

Robby grabbed the armor suit by the gauntlet.

Nothing happened.

Not knowing what else to do, Robby gave the armored hand a handshake.

There came a deafening *boom!* and a blinding flash of white light. It took Robby a moment to realize it, but now *he* was wearing the armor. Yes, he could feel the padded undersuit and the chainmail and the heavy armor plates. He could feel the chin strap of the helmet and the leather gloves beneath the iron gauntlets. And it all seemed to fit perfectly.

An authentic medieval suit of armor!

However, in another moment, Robby felt another, more-distressing sensation.

He could not move.

Not at all. He couldn't move a finger or wriggle a toe. He was totally immobilized. And he couldn't see very well, because there was only the slot in the helmet to see out of. However, through the slot, he saw another boy in the gallery, just on the other side of the velvet rope, where Robby himself had stood only an instant before.

The boy was about Robby's size and he seemed very relieved about something. He was looking at himself and laughing. He looked down at his arms and legs, and he happily stretched and bent himself as though he'd gone a long time without moving.

Then the boy looked at Robby. Or rather, he peered through the slot of the helmet, just as Robby had done. The strange boy made a slight bow and sarcastically whispered, "Thank you! Now it is *your* turn."

Then he vanished.

Robby tried to move. He tried to walk. He tried screaming, tried calling out for his mother, father, and even his sister. Robby suddenly wished for nothing more than to be with them. He would look at every dumb old painting in every dumb old museum on earth if he could only be out of this armor and with them again.

But it was no use. He was paralyzed and silenced. He could not scream. He tried and tried, and he perhaps moved just slightly, but not enough to be noticed—not even by someone who was looking his way. A feeling came over Robby that instead of wearing the amazing suit of armor for only a few minutes, he'd be wearing it for a long, long time. All he could really do was stare out from behind his visor.

It was six o'clock.

The museum was emptying. All the museum-goers were leaving. All of them, that is, except one family. It was a mother, father, and daughter, and they dashed from gallery to gallery, searching desperately for someone. At last they came to the information desk.

"We've lost our son," said Robby's mother. Her voice quavered with anxiety. "He's about this tall. He has black hair and brown eyes and he's wearing a green t-shirt!"

Robby's father added, "His name is Robby. He told us he was going to the gallery where there are swords and armor and knights."

The museum worker looked puzzled. "Are you

sure he didn't already leave the museum?" she asked. "Might he have gone home on his own?"

"No," said Robby's mother. "We live an hour's drive away."

"I see," said the museum worker, now wearing a look of grave concern. "Of course we'll search the entire museum. But we've had no reports of any lost children all day, and—this is the odd thing—this museum has *no* galleries with armor or swords or anything like that."

CHAPTER 4
BEDROOM IN THE CELLAR

As she lay shivering in the darkness, Whitney Brittle decided that she was never coming back to Idaho. It was freezing cold in Idaho. It was muddy, snowy, and damp in Idaho, and a raw wind seemed to always blow.

Whitney should not have been surprised. After all, it was the night before Thanksgiving. Idaho was *always* this way the night before Thanksgiving. This was the way everyone in Idaho expected Idaho to *be*.

But this was the first time Whitney had ever been to Idaho. She was eleven years old and lived in San Diego, where it was always warm, so it hadn't really occurred to her that there were places which were so freezing cold. In San Diego it was just about always sunny, it never snowed, and the temperature rarely dipped below 60 degrees, even at night in the middle of winter! Whitney was also what her mother called "slight of build." In other words, Whitney was very skinny, which made it difficult for her to stay warm.

Whitney and her older sister, Ellen, had come to Idaho a few days earlier with their parents to visit their Uncle Reggie and Aunt Nancy for Thanksgiving. Reggie and Nancy lived in a big farmhouse upon what appeared to be an endless stretch of potato fields. However, there were no potatoes growing at that time of the year, and there weren't many trees or anything else in the area, and so it seemed more like Reggie and Nancy lived on an endless windy stretch of snow-covered *mud*.

You couldn't even call it "the middle of nowhere," because the *middle* of most places is usually where you find the most interesting things. There was nothing interesting here—no beaches, no cool pizza places, nowhere to shop or skateboard. Reggie and Nancy's potato farm was more like the boring, lower left-hand corner of nowhere.

And so Whitney tugged the quilt up over her head and tried to sleep by promising herself over and over that she'd never return to this barren and frozen wasteland.

This wasn't the first time someone felt this way about Idaho, of course, but it wasn't *all* bad. Whitney's aunt and uncle were very nice, and they'd invited about fifty other relatives to celebrate Thanksgiving, too. By Whitney's count, there were five grandparents, six aunts, four uncles and, somewhere in this great flock of humanity, she even found a *great*-grandmother.

And there were dozens of cousins.

First cousins, second cousins—some of them once removed, some twice. Whitney had no idea what it meant to be a "first cousin, twice removed," but the cousins were always up to something fun— card games, video games, board games. There was football to watch on TV, and if someone wanted to actually *play* football, ten or twelve cousins were always willing.

In the evenings, Uncle Reggie would build a big fire and sit by the fireplace to tell scary stories. He told the tale of the Wendigo, an evil spirit that haunted the wastelands of the frozen north. He told the one about the farmer who locked himself in his own basement every full moon because he was secretly a werewolf. And he told the urban legend of the mass-murderer with a hook for a hand, who stalked his victims along lonesome country roads.

Then Aunt Nancy would stir up a big batch of hot cocoa. Whitney wasn't a big fan of scary stories, but she huddled close to the fire and guzzled about a gallon of the cocoa, trying to warm up for bedtime. This really was the only thing that bothered Whitney Brittle about Idaho—the nights were just so *cold*.

With so many people staying at Nancy and Reggie's house, it was quite crowded at night. Relatives bedded down in every room and on every square-foot of floor. Whitney's parents were assigned to a small bed in one of the spare bedrooms upstairs, while Whitney and her sister were sent to the bedroom in the cellar. It had a bare concrete floor, just one small window, and a heavy door that locked with an old-fashioned skeleton key.

"Wow, spooky!" said Whitney when she first saw the room.

"Yeah," said Ellen, "It's like a dungeon in a castle!"

Later on, they realized the room also had no heater vents, and at night it got as cold as a walk-in refrigerator. Still, the two sisters counted themselves lucky to at least have a bed, instead of a sleeping bag on a hard patch of floor. They'd heard that one of their uncles had to sleep in a *bathtub*.

The first two nights weren't bad. Ellen wasn't quite so skinny as Whitney, and her body heat helped keep the bed somewhat warm. But now, in the frosty chill of the night before Thanksgiving, Whitney felt differently.

She'd just been awoken by the sound of her own chattering teeth.

Ellen had helped herself to *all* the covers, including the sheet. Whitney could certainly understand why—this was the coldest night yet. But Whitney felt she might perish without at least some kind of covering. She wore pajamas, yes, but not the warm, woolly kind. These were light and thin San Diego-style pajamas, and the icy Idaho air passed right through them. Ellen was also taking up way more than her share of the bed. And so Whitney clung to the edge of the mattress, frozen from nose to toes.

"Ellen," Whitney muttered, her teeth clacking miserably, "g-gimme some b-blankets."

Ellen didn't respond, so Whitney groped around in the dark for some small edge or corner of the bed covers. The moon was big and full that night, but not much moonlight came through the tiny, prison-cell window. Whitney somehow got hold of a fistful of blanket from Ellen's side of the bed and pulled it over. This barely covered Whitney's shoulders and legs, but it was better than freezing to death.

A moment later, the covers were snatched back to Ellen's side, and Whitney was left in the cold again.

"Ellen!" she hissed. "Quit hogging all the blankets! And shove over!"

There came only a sort of snoring growl from Ellen's side of the bed. Whitney had never heard her sister snore that way, but she was too cold to worry about it. She felt around again, grabbed the covers, and pulled hard. This time, however, the blankets didn't budge.

"She must have the covers tucked in under herself," thought Whitney. "Two can play that game."

Whitney grabbed the blanket with both hands and rolled herself over, using the weight of her body (which wasn't much) to crank some covers onto her side. When she was covered up, Whitney hastily tucked the blanket under her body.

"There!" grumbled Whitney. "Now quit hogging!"

But the covers were torn right back off again—effortlessly—as if Whitney wasn't even there. This was getting ridiculous. Whitney blew into her hands to warm them. She was so cold, so tired.

"Listen, Ellen," she said through chattering teeth, "if you c-c-can't share the bed, I'm gonna go tell Mom and Dad to make you sleep in a b-bathtub!"

Whitney heard nothing but a little more grumbling or growling. It was almost as if Ellen were guarding her territory like some mean old dog. No matter. Whitney climbed out of the bed, groped in the dark for the covers, and gave them a great heave.

But before Whitney had retrieved even two feet of the blanket, it was wrenched back so violently that Whitney fell back into the bed. It was like being pulled by a tow truck.

"That's it!" cried Whitney, getting out of the bed.

As she groped her way across the dark room, Whitney had to admit that she was impressed with how strong Ellen had apparently gotten, but now Whitney was sleepy, freezing cold, and angry.

"I'm telling Mom and Dad!" Whitney grumbled, and she went out.

To get upstairs from the cellar bedroom, Whitney had only to walk out of the bedroom door, cross a narrow hallway, and then head straight up the cellar stairs. She couldn't decide whether to stomp angrily up the stairs or tip-toe to avoid waking any of her numerous relations. So, she tried to do both at the same time, resulting in a comical sort of "Frankenstein walk."

When she got upstairs, she found Ellen sitting at the kitchen table.

Whitney stared at Ellen for several seconds. Their parents were at the table, too. Whitney stared at them for a while. They were all sipping hot cocoa. Whitney blinked as though she didn't understand what she was seeing.

"Mom! Dad!" she said in a harsh whisper. She pointed an accusing finger at Ellen. "I'm freezing and exhausted because Ellen is a flagrant blanket thief!"

"Keep your voice down," said Whitney's dad quietly. "People are sleeping."

"That's what *I'm* trying to do!" Whitney insisted. "But *she* keeps taking all the covers!"

"What are you talking about?" said Ellen with a frown. She took a gulp of cocoa. "I've been sitting here for an hour or more."

"Yeah," said Whitney's mom, nodding. "Ellen told us that Uncle Reggie's big dog climbed into your bed a while ago and there wasn't enough room for the three of you."

"And your mom and I couldn't sleep, either," added Whitney's dad, "so, we're having some cocoa. Want some?"

Something about these revelations made even less sense than seeing Ellen in the kitchen when Whitney had just barely left her in the cellar all wrapped up in the covers.

"First of all," said Whitney, "Uncle Reggie's dog *isn't* big. Secondly, Uncle Reggie's dog *isn't* downstairs. Uncle Reggie's dog is right over *there*."

Whitney pointed at the friendly little sheepdog, who was curled up by the fireplace. The dog seemed to somehow sense he had been spoken of. The friendly pooch raised his head and wagged his tail. The others looked confused by this but had to agree that the dog certainly was *not* big and was very much *not* downstairs.

"*Ellen* is the one who's downstairs hogging the whole bed!" said Whitney.

His mom and dad looked at Ellen with deeply skeptical looks on their faces.

A realization was dawning on Whitney, too. Blinking and scratching her head, she returned to the top of the cellar staircase. There was just enough moonlight to see down the stairs. The cellar bedroom door stood partly open, but just at that moment, an arm covered with gray fur emerged from the darkened bedroom doorway. At the end of the hairy arm was an equally hairy hand or paw, each finger of which was tipped with a long, sharp claw. Whitney heard a deep, sleepy, growl, and then the hand or paw or whatever it was grabbed the doorknob and pulled the door shut.

Whitney gasped. Her eyes grew wide and her mouth dropped open.

The old-fashion lock creaked creepily and then clacked into place. A moment later, a skeleton key slid out from beneath the door with a soft metallic rasping sound, and whoever—or *whatev*er—was in that frigid cellar bedroom was now locked in for the night.

CHAPTER 5
THE SECRET OF OLIVER WHISTLER

OLIVER WHISTLER WAS about your age, I would guess, with a mop of dark hair and a friendly smile. He was generally kind, polite, and easy to get along with. Sports didn't interest Oliver, but he was a valued member of the chess club, and he had many friends. Everyone thought of him as a "good kid."

If you knew Oliver, if you were his next-door neighbor or school-chum, you'd assume that Oliver was happy and carefree.

But Oliver Whistler was *not* carefree.

In fact, Oliver was the opposite of carefree. One might guess that the opposite of the word "carefree" is "care*ful*," because it seems like "careful" should mean "*full* of *cares*." But you know that's not the case, because of course "careful" means "cautious, taking special care."

The opposite of "carefree" is actually the word "care*worn*." This is a very good word to describe Oliver because he was *worn down* by his cares and worries.

Oliver did a fine job of hiding this. At school, he joked and laughed with friends. At home, he helped his mother set the table for supper, and he helped his father fix things around the house. On the outside, Oliver seemed normal and happy.

On the inside he was miserable.

I'm sure you want to know *why* Oliver was so unhappy. We'll come to that shortly, but first I'd like to say that Oliver was not merely unhappy. We're all unhappy at times. Maybe someone says an unkind word to you at school, or maybe you don't get exactly what you wanted for your birthday. Such things can make us temporarily unhappy. However, it's quite a different thing to be miserable all the time, and then have to hide it from everyone.

You see, Oliver had a secret. It was a terrible secret, and if you know anything at all about terrible secrets, you know that they have a way of taking on a life of their own. And this is what was about to happen to Oliver—his secret was about to escape his control.

One day, Oliver's friend Ethan said, "Hey, Oliver, there's a carnival coming to town tomorrow. Let's go after school."

"No thanks," Oliver answered glumly.

"Why not?" asked Ethan. "They're gonna have rides and games and food, and they've got a giant gorilla. C'mon! It'll be fun!"

Oliver considered this. "Maybe he's right," thought Oliver. "Maybe it'll take my mind off"—but he didn't finish his thought.

"Okay," said Oliver with a shrug, "I'll go."

On Thursday, Oliver met Ethan after school and they set out on their bikes. It was nearly Halloween, and although it was a warm afternoon, the daylight was fading fast. As he pedaled along, Oliver saw the glow of carnival lights above the trees and houses. Suddenly, he wanted to turn his bike around and go home. He nearly did. The carnival seemed to call out to Oliver, to invite him, but not in a good way. It felt more like being called to the principal's office at school.

"What's the matter?" asked Ethan. "Why are you slowing down?"

"Who, me?" asked Oliver. "Oh, my back tire is a little low on air."

Soon they reached the carnival. It was set up in a harvested cornfield on the edge of town. The cornstalk stubble made crunching noises beneath their bicycle tires. They came to a ticket booth. It was small but brightly painted, with a high roof and fancy carving around the gables. Ethan went to the ticket window and paid his admission.

Next, Oliver stepped up to the booth. A weird, purple light came from within. Inside there was a man wearing a worn-out-top hat and a pair of what looked like sunglasses. The lenses were round and mirrored, and Oliver saw a reflection of himself in each lens.

The man took Oliver's money and grinned. Like the glaring carnival lights, the man's smile made Oliver uneasy. The man said nothing. He only tipped his shabby hat and gestured for Oliver to enter.

On the carnival grounds there were rides and food vendors and lots of people. There were jugglers and fire-eaters. Along the midway, Oliver saw the carnival games, such as knocking down milk bottles with a baseball to win a teddy bear, or shooting tin ducks with a water gun to win a toy airplane. The autumn air carried the odors of popcorn and the sounds of laughter.

Oliver caught sight of the cage where the ape was kept. The beast was indeed massive. People stood around gawking and pointing while the ape sat slouching in the middle of the cage. The creature looked very bored. However, when the ape saw Oliver, it sat upright, as if it recognized Oliver. The great beast stood up and came to the bars, watching Oliver closely. Oliver hurried along.

"Let's go on the tilt-o-whirl!" cried Ethan, pointing. "No, let's get a caramel apple first and *then* go on the tilt-o-whirl!"

This seemed like the wrong order in which to do those things, but Oliver was eager to pass by the ape, and so he hurried along behind Ethan. The caramel apple was not ripe, and it was very tart. The sun was setting. The flaring of the lights made Oliver feel dizzy and lost. He wanted to go home.

"Come on!" cried Ethan. "To the tilt-o-whirl!"

They rode the tilt-o-whirl, which made Oliver queasy. Ethan dragged him onward, but Oliver felt more and more sick.

"Let's go on the Ferris wheel," said Ethan.

"You go ahead," said Oliver, holding up one hand. "I've got an upset stomach."

"Aw, come on," Ethan insisted.

"No, I need to sit down," said Oliver. "You go and meet me back here when you're done."

"Suit yourself," said Ethan, scampering away.

Although the evening was cooler now, Oliver was clammy with sweat. He found himself outside the tent of the fortune teller. The tent was small, probably large enough for only two people inside. It was embroidered with strange golden stars, moons, and other markings. Across the tent's front opening hung a shabby purple silk curtain.

A sign on the tent read, *Fortunes Told: $1*, but despite what most people would consider a *very* reasonable fee, Oliver had no interest in having his fortune told. What he wanted was to rest, and beside the tent sat a small bench. As quietly as he could manage, Oliver crept to the bench and lay down on it.

"Come in," said a voice from inside the tent. It was an old woman's voice, high-pitched and creaky.

Oliver ignored it. He slumped on the bench, his head on the armrest and his eyes shut.

"Did you hear me?" It was the creaky voice again. "I said you may come in now."

Oliver rose to leave, but as he did, the purple silk curtain drew aside. A reddish light shone within.

Oliver froze. In the tent, an old woman sat on a stool. It was the fortune teller. Her face was wrinkled, her eyes were cloudy, and her nose was long and pointed. She was dressed all in black, and on her head she wore a black head scarf.

She looked at Oliver. He took a step backward. She smiled, then raised her hand and waved at Oliver to come inside.

Oliver got ready to run, but before he did, the old woman demanded, "Oliver Whistler. Come inside, *now*."

As though pulled by invisible wires, Oliver went to the tent and stood at the opening. A lantern hung from the ceiling of the tent, casting a reddish light. There was no one in the tent but the old fortune teller. Oliver stepped inside, wondering who might have drawn back the curtain, because the old woman sat at a small table, not close enough to reach the curtain. Upon the table sat something round and perhaps the size of a grapefruit but covered by a black cloth.

The fortune teller gestured at the stool on the opposite side of the table and said, "Sit."

Oliver sat.

"Do you know why you're here?" asked the old woman.

Oliver shook his head.

"Yes, you do," she answered.

"Yes, I do," he thought.

The fortune teller lifted the black cloth to reveal a crystal ball.

Oliver stared at it. He couldn't look away. It was as clear as pure water, and yet at its center there was a cloud of black mist that spun like a tiny hurricane. Oliver leaned closer.

"That's right," said the old woman. "Look."

Oliver gazed deeply into the crystal sphere. Within the spinning mist, Oliver saw lights and shapes. Suddenly, he saw himself at home and going to school. He saw himself with his friends and parents.

And he saw his secret.

He drew back in horror.

"Ahh," said the old woman, holding up a gnarled finger. "You are hiding something, young man."

Oliver felt awful, and it had nothing to do with the under-ripe caramel apple or the tilt-o-whirl. His stomach lurched and his heart slammed within him. He wanted to cover the glass ball. He wanted to run and hide. For there was his secret, as plain as day:

Oliver Whistler was a cheater.

He'd never wanted to be a cheater, never

planned to be a cheater. It just sort of happened during the previous school year, when Oliver found himself one day in math class completely unprepared for a midterm test.

Let me say that Oliver was not bad at math. He received generally good grades in all his classes. He'd simply forgotten about the math test and had not studied. It happens.

Oliver glanced around the classroom, wondering what to do, and his eyes happened to fall on the test of the person seated to his left. He'd never forget whose test it was—it was Jessica Cortez's test. She was already halfway done with the first page, working out the math problems quickly and efficiently. And what neat and clear handwriting she had! Without thinking, Oliver began copying Jessica's answers onto his own test.

But then Jessica turned to the next page.

Again, Oliver panicked. He hadn't been able to copy down all the answers, so he turned to the person on his right. This was Randy Bartlet. Randy was still working on the first page, and so Oliver copied down Randy's answers.

Why didn't anyone catch Oliver cheating? Perhaps the teacher was distracted, and the students were probably too absorbed in the test to notice.

Maybe Oliver was just really good at glancing at someone else's work without attracting attention.

All we can say for certain is that Oliver got away with it.

He didn't feel good about this. In fact, Oliver felt terrible about the "A" he received on that math test. He stayed up at night worrying about it. Every day, he considered confessing. It was practically all he thought about.

But then, suddenly, it was time for his midterm *science* test, and he'd been so preoccupied worrying about the math test, he'd neglected to study *again*. There he was, staring hopelessly at a midterm, and once again he panicked. This time he peeked at Ganesh Kumar's paper on the left and Simone Dupont's work on the right.

He got away with cheating on *that* test, too.

It got worse, which is to say Oliver got better at cheating. By the end of the school year, Oliver was cheating on most tests *and* his homework. And every time he cheated, it became more difficult to confess or even stop.

Now a new school year had begun, and Oliver not only copied test answers and homework from neighboring students, he also wrote useful facts and figures on his wrists and arms and ankles, up under his sleeves and socks, so that he didn't have to memorize anything. He'd even figured out how to sneak into his classrooms during lunchtime and find test answers in the teacher's textbooks.

"Oliver Whistler!" cried the old fortune teller, her voice shrill. "Your time has come!"

Oliver stared at the old woman. Her eyes were pale and hazy, as though she were partially blind, but Oliver knew she saw deep into his heart, where his secret lay hidden. He thought about confessing. He thought about telling his parents and all his teachers —and last year's teachers. The principal and school counselor would have to be told, too, and maybe all the people he'd cheated from. What would his friends Jessica, Randy, Ganesh, and Simone say? Would he be suspended from school? Would he have to go back and redo all of last year's schoolwork?

"I can't!" cried Oliver. "I just can't!"

The fortune teller closed her eyes and nodded once. "Then your secret shall destroy you," she murmured. "It will grow larger and more fearsome. And when it is strong enough, it will break free. Is this what you want?"

Oliver's face was slick with sweat. "No," he whispered.

"Then confess, Oliver Whistler!" cried the old fortune teller. "Confess or meet your doom!"

Oliver ran out of the tent. Behind him, he heard the fortune teller cackling. He ran through the crowds of happy people and between the carnival rides. He ran and ran, but still he heard the fortune teller's laughter.

He ran past the gorilla's cage and again caught sight of the beast. Had it grown *larger*? When the ape saw Oliver, it sprang to its feet, slamming against the bars of the cage, roaring savagely, and grasping at Oliver through the bars. Oliver raced on. In the shadows and winking lights, Oliver somehow found the ticket booth, retrieved his bike, and plunged blindly into the night.

The next morning, Oliver awoke in his bed. He lay on his back blinking awhile, his mind a jumble. Sunlight streamed in through his bedroom window, and a soft, friendly voice floated into the room.

"Ollie? Are you awake?" It was his mother calling him from the kitchen. "Wake up, Ollie. You'll be late for school."

Oliver thought about the night before. He'd gone to the carnival with Ethan. He ate a caramel apple and rode on the tilt-o-whirl. But what about the rest?

The old woman and the crystal ball and the giant gorilla? Was it real?

He got out of bed and wasted no time getting dressed.

"Oh, good," said his mother as Oliver passed through the kitchen. "I thought you were going to be late. Hey, wait! What about your breakfast?"

Oliver shook his head and muttered a hasty goodbye. Then he shrugged on his backpack, hopped on his bike, and sped away to school. When he arrived, he ran straight to his math classroom. His math teacher, Ms. Lovelace, sat at her desk.

"Oliver," she said. "Good morning."

Oliver was out of breath. "Hi," he panted. "I—I— I need to—"

"You need to catch your breath?" joked Ms. Lovelace.

Oliver's confession stood on the end of his tongue, but he was filled with dread and guilt.

"You know," said Ms. Lovelace, "I've been meaning to tell you that I'm quite pleased with your test scores this year."

"I—I need to—" Oliver stammered. He was imagining telling Ms. Lovelace about his cheating. He thought about all the tests and homework he'd cheated on. He imagined repeating the confession to all his other teachers, his parents, and his friends.

He couldn't. It would be too embarrassing, too humiliating.

Ms. Lovelace waited patiently for Oliver to finish.

"I need to—to—to—*to give you my homework*," he blurted at last.

"Oh," said his teacher. "You might have waited until class, but, very well."

Oliver clawed in his backpack and handed over the homework. Then he bolted from the classroom and out of the school.

All that day, Oliver wandered through town on his bike. He rode to the duck pond and up to Lookout Hill. He wandered down to the railroad tracks and over to the city swimming pool, which had been drained and locked up for the year. All the while Oliver thought only of the astonishingly poor decisions he'd made lately, and if he might undo them.

But Oliver's heart had grown cold.

"I don't have to tell anyone about this," Oliver decided. He spat on the ground. "It's my own private business. I'm not hurting anyone. Why do I have to know math and science and English, anyhow? No one can make me tell, and no one can make me stop."

When Oliver came to this conclusion, he looked up. It was late afternoon. The sky was gold and purple. And he was at the carnival ticket booth once more.

The man in the shabby top hat watched Oliver from behind his mirrored spectacles. Oliver saw the two reflections of himself. They looked tired and tormented and ill. But the ticket booth man smiled at him and raised one eyebrow, as if inviting him back again.

Oliver reached into his pocket, removed a handful of money, and flung it through the ticket booth window. Then he stormed ahead without looking back. It was a Friday evening, and the carnival was packed with people. Oliver shoved his way through the crowd, huffing and snarling as he went. He blustered past the Ferris wheel and the tilt-o-whirl. He stomped past the games and the food huts.

Soon he stood outside the fortune teller's tent.

The purple curtain drew back, and the fortune teller looked up from her crystal ball. The lantern inside flared ominously. Oliver held the old woman in his angry gaze. She gestured for him to sit, but he didn't. He stayed outside, taking not a single step toward the tent.

"You can't tell me what to do," sneered Oliver, jabbing a finger at her. "It's *my* business. It's my own *private* business!"

The old woman closed her eyes and nodded once. The purple curtain fell closed across the opening of the tent, and a chill came over Oliver. His anger fled and was replaced by loneliness and fear. He ran to the tent and tore the curtain aside.

But the tent was empty. No lantern, no table, no crystal ball, and no fortune teller.

Oliver backed away, stumbling.

"Good," he whispered to himself. "She's gone."

He turned and wandered back through the surging carnival crowd, through the people and music and glittering lights.

Then, without meaning to, Oliver came to the gorilla's cage, and he was sure it was at least twice as large as it had been the night before. The thing barely fit inside its cage. Oliver hunched his shoulders and looked away, hoping the ape would not see him.

But this didn't work.

The massive ape saw Oliver, and it again crashed against the bars and groped for him. The spectators gasped and backed away. The cage shook terribly, and the ape bellowed with fury. Oliver side-glanced and locked eyes with the ape. This enraged the beast more. It grabbed the bars and yanked them apart as if they'd been made of licorice whips. The beast had broken free.

And it immediately came after Oliver.

Carnival-goers screamed and ran in every direction. The ape's handlers tried to recapture it but were hurled back one by one. This gave Oliver a slight head-start. He darted between people and behind the tents. It was getting dark and the carnival lights cast crazy shadows. The ape charged after Oliver, but it kept losing sight of him, so it paused now and then to look around before charging onward. The creature knocked people down, leaped over food huts, and tore through tents. Oliver ran as fast as he could, but he heard the monster howling behind him, and it got closer every moment.

Somehow, Oliver slipped away from the carnival and into the night. The ape must have lost sight of Oliver again; it was no longer behind him. Oliver clambered over fences, ran through farm fields, and hopped over a small creek. He ran for what seemed like miles. Then he reached the cover of the foothill forest south of town. It was very dark there.

Exhausted, Oliver threw himself onto the ground behind a tall tree.

When he'd caught his breath, Oliver peeked around the tree trunk. He saw the carnival in the distance, but he couldn't see the great monster. He scanned the darkness, his heart thrumming in his chest.

Then he saw movement.

Yes, there it was. An enormous, shadowy shape coming along the way Oliver had come. Was it even *larger* now? It stormed across the farm fields. It ripped through the fences. Then it stopped and searched the tree line of the forest. It was close enough that Oliver could hear its snorting breath. Faint starlight glimmered in the monster's eyes, two pinpoints of light.

And then its gaze fell upon Oliver.

What happened next is a matter of public record. You can look it up in any newspaper archive. On Saturday morning, the local media reported that a young boy had gone missing. *Local Boy Vanishes without Trace*, read the headline. The report claimed the boy had been seen early on Friday at school but had not shown up for any classes. The police didn't have many clues, but they seemed confident they'd find him.

The second story was about a captive gorilla that escaped from a visiting carnival. *Giant Ape Escapes Carnival*, read the much-smaller headline. The press reported the great captive creature had torn open its cage, caused quite a bit of property damage, and then disappeared into the woods south of town.

No trace of the boy nor the ape were ever found.

CHAPTER 6

THE NIGHT BEAST OF CROOKED CANYON

IT HAD BEEN what Graham Amberson called "a really groovy, super-fun day."

Graham and his family had spent all Saturday in Billings shopping for Christmas presents. And it was very good that they had so much fun that day, rushing from shop to shop and enjoying Christmas festivities, because their evening was going to be a total holiday nightmare.

Billings was a big town in Montana where the Ambersons went if they wanted to shop for something special or have dinner at a nice restaurant. The drive to Billings took more than an hour, because their mother had to drive up and over a high mountain pass called Crooked Canyon.

But it was worth it. Graham had finished all his

Christmas shopping. He bought a pair of fur-lined gloves for his mother, Janelle. At the mall, Graham found a video game (on sale!) for his big brother, Bryan. And at the toy store, he'd picked out a nifty stuffed unicorn for his younger sister, Addison (whom everybody called Addy).

Graham had blown his entire savings, but it was all for Christmas, so he felt great. He also knew that his mother had bought presents for all the kids, too, but she'd cleverly brought along black garbage bags to conceal them.

"If you peek at these presents," Janelle warned the kids with a laugh, as she put the bags in the back of the SUV and shut the tailgate, "I'll return them all to the stores and you'll get nothing but socks and underwear for Christmas!"

Graham was eleven years old and lived with his family out in the Montana countryside. Addy was only seven. Their older brother Bryan wasn't a kid anymore—he was nineteen and went to college in Ohio. He'd come back home for Christmas break.

That morning, when the Amberson family had piled into their SUV for the drive to Billings, the weather had been beautiful. Christmas was only a week away, and snow covered the ground, but it was one of those warm winter days when the sky is bright blue, the air is calm, and it's warm enough outside to leave your coat at home.

After the Christmas shopping, they'd stopped at Pizza Ranch, one of their favorite restaurants. They ordered an extra-large, deep-dish pizza with about twenty toppings, then relaxed while they waited.

"Hey, Mom," said Graham, "can I have some quarters to play video games?"

"Sure," said Janelle, reaching for her purse, "but you have to share them with Addy."

They played two games of Space Evaders and three games of Bonkey Kong before the pizza arrived. It was delicious. Graham ate three humongous slices and drank two big glasses of root beer. By the time they got up to leave, Graham was belching sleepily and ready for a nap on the ride home.

However, when they left Pizza Ranch, they saw that the weather had turned very sour. The once-clear sky was now gray and gloomy, and it was snowing hard.

Also, Graham knew it would be dark soon, and they'd have to go back through Crooked Canyon.

Instead of feeling slightly sleepy, Graham now felt very queasy. He got into the SUV, fastened his seatbelt, and said, "Hey, Addy. Don't forget to buckle up."

The road through Crooked Canyon was narrow and, well, *crooked*, twisting and climbing crazily through a forested mountain wilderness. To one side of the road was a cliff wall of rock, and on the other side there were drop-offs into deep ravines. Crooked Canyon also had a reputation for being wild, full of wolves and bears and other beasts. The drive through Crooked Canyon was always just slightly scary during the daytime, in good weather.

But at night in foul weather, Crooked Canyon was terrifying.

Janelle looked at the stormy sky as she climbed into the SUV. There was worry in her eyes. Bryan looked worried, too. The pizza and root beer gurgled in Graham's stomach. Only Addy seemed to have no worries—she was too young to know how dangerous snowy Montana canyons could be.

Janelle sat in the driver's seat, of course, and Bryan sat beside her in the passenger seat. Addy sat behind Janelle, and Graham sat behind Bryan.

It was pitch-black outside before they ever reached Crooked Canyon, and the winter storm had gathered in strength. The SUV's windshield wipers struggled to keep up with the pelting snow. Before the wipers were able to sweep over and back across the windshield, it was already covered with snow again.

Graham's mother never drove faster than the speed limit, but going too slow could be dangerous, too. Other cars and trucks on the highway were hissing past at frightening speeds.

"I wish everyone would slow down," murmured Janelle, her voice tense.

Ka-fwomp, ka-fwomp, ka-fwomp, went the wipers.

They soon reached the summit, the highest part of the canyon. From his seat behind Bryan, Graham craned his neck to see the road. Heavy snow was falling, and even on the fastest setting, the wipers just couldn't keep the snow off. And so Graham caught only short flashes of the stormy blackness and the snow piling up on the roadway.

On the way to Billings that morning, Mom and Bryan were talking and laughing. Mom had asked Bryan questions about college, and Bryan replied with funny stories about his classes and roommates. Now both were deathly quiet. If they spoke at all, it was about the driving conditions.

"I can hardly see a thing," grumbled Janelle.

Ka-fwomp, ka-fwomp, ka-fwomp.

"I'm glad you're driving and not me," said Bryan.

Addy acted as though nothing were out of the ordinary. She hummed tunelessly and played a game on her video tablet. Somehow, this made Graham more nervous. He peered out the side windows, but snow was sticking to them, and it was totally dark outside, anyway. According to the clock on Graham's wrist-phone, they'd been driving for an hour already and should be getting close to home.

"Are we almost there?" asked Graham.

"No," said his mother. "It's taking longer because we're driving so slowly."

"How much longer?" asked Graham.

"Graham," said Bryan, "Mom can't talk right now. Don't worry. She's a good driver. We'll be home soon."

All at once, a monstrous, noisy thing pulled alongside the SUV. It made a deafening roar and sent a wave of solid snow crashing across the SUV's hood and windshield.

It was a snowplow, the kind that drove back and forth through mountain canyons during snowstorms. It was basically a massive orange dump truck with a giant, shovel-like push-blade on the front. In the back it carried salt and sand to make the roads less slick.

The snowplow was passing them on the left. Graham's mother yelped as the plow practically buried them in an avalanche of snow. The SUV shuddered and swerved. The windshield wipers didn't stand a chance, and for a moment, Graham's mother was driving blind. She gripped the steering wheel, fighting for control. Even Addy looked up from her tablet, slightly alarmed.

And then the snowplow passed on ahead.

"We're all right!" said Janelle, glancing at the kids in the rear-view mirror. "Everything's fine. Just a snowplow. And look, the road is much clearer now that we're behind it."

Graham looked, and through the snow and *ka-fwomp*ing wipers, he saw that the plow had indeed cleared the road. He eased back in his seat, thinking that maybe everything would be okay after all.

But then something enormous and beastly loomed for an instant in the headlights. It was a blur of dark fur, claws, and a single huge red-glaring eye. Janelle slammed on the brakes. The SUV spun in dizzying circles. Graham was thrown hard against his seatbelt. Everyone screamed. Graham just knew they'd be hurled over the guardrail and down the ravine.

And then everything was quiet and still again.

Everything except the *ka-fwomp* of the wipers.

The SUV was stopped by the side of the highway, next to the guardrail that kept them from tumbling down into the canyon.

"Everyone all right?" shouted Janelle, her voice shaky. "Graham? Addy? Anyone hurt?"

"No," said Graham.

"Yes," said Addy.

Bryan turned around in his seat. "No, you're not all right? Or yes, you're hurt?"

"We're okay," said Graham and Addy together.

"What *was* that thing?" asked Graham, "A deer?"

"No," said Bryan.

"It was way bigger than a deer," said Janelle. "It was bigger than our car."

"Was it a bear? Did we hit it?" asked Graham.

"Yeah, I think so," said Janelle. "But everything happened so fast. You guys stay here for a sec. I'll go check."

"I'll go with you," said Bryan.

"No, Bryan," said Janelle. "You stay here with them."

"Okay," said Bryan.

"No!" said Graham. "Don't go, Mom! You'll be hit by a car! Or that thing out there will get you!"

"Graham, don't be silly," his mother replied.

"Nothing's gonna *get me*. I gotta find out if we can still drive."

A few cars and trucks sped past, hissing noisily over the wet and snowy road, but none of them seemed dangerously close, so Janelle unbuckled her seat belt and opened the door. The interior light came on in the SUV, casting a dreadful shadow on Janelle's face.

"Be careful, Mom," said Bryan.

Janelle nodded and stepped out into the darkness. The door thunked closed. The SUV was still running, and the wipers *ka-fwomp*ed across the windshield.

"Bryan," said Graham timidly, "what the heck did we hit?"

"Honestly?" he answered, "all I saw was a wall of fur. I think I saw an eye."

"Did you see horns?" Graham asked. "Or fangs? I saw claws and fangs."

"Yeah, I think so," said Bryan. "I don't know."

"Look," cried Addy, "there's mom!"

In the brief, shadowy glimpses between the constant sweeping of the wipers, they watched her stooping to examine the front of the SUV.

And then she vanished.

One moment she was there in the weird light of

the headlights. Then the wipers swept over the windshield, and then she was gone.

"Where'd she go?" said Bryan sitting up straight. With the palm of his hand, he tried to wipe some of the fog from the inside of the window, but it didn't help. Their mother was definitely not in front of the SUV.

"That *thing* took her!" cried Graham. "The night-beast! It got her!"

"Graham," said Bryan, "settle down. Maybe she just slipped in the snow. I'll go help her." He unbuckled his seatbelt.

"No!" Graham shouted. "It'll take you, too!"

"Don't panic," said Bryan, holding up a hand. "I'll be right back."

This should have made Graham feel better. Bryan was much older than Graham. He was smart and basically a grown-up. But the night-beast was out there.

Bryan opened the passenger-side door, and the interior light came on inside the SUV again, throwing the same spooky, doomed shadow on Bryan's face. He went out and shut the door behind him.

Just as before, Graham and Addy saw Bryan in front of the SUV. He appeared to be looking for footprints in the snow left by their mother. The wipers swished back and forth over the windshield, trying and failing to clear away the snow.

And just as before, Bryan disappeared, too.

"I knew it!" Graham released himself from his seatbelt and scrambled up to the front of the vehicle. Bryan was nowhere to be seen, and snow covered the other windows, but Graham nevertheless *sensed* something moving around the SUV, first on one side, then the other, and maybe even above. It had to be the night-beast with its horns, tusks, and burning red eye.

"Graham!" shouted Addy.

"Not now, Addy!" replied Graham, looking wildly out the windshield.

"Graham," Addy repeated, "call him!"

"Call who?" cried Graham, his voice squeaky with panic.

"Call Bryan!" said Addy. "With your phone!"

"Oh, yeah!" said Graham. He could call Bryan's cell phone. "Great idea, Gab," he said. And so he pressed a button on his wrist phone, scrolled to Bryan's number, and hit the *CALL* button.

They heard Bryan's phone ringing and vibrating, and they saw it light up. It was on the dashboard of the SUV, plugged into a charger.

"He didn't take it with him," said Graham, panicking again.

"Try mom's phone!"

Graham nodded and quickly called his mother's phone.

Through the tiny speaker of the wrist-phone, they heard a few rings, and then, "Hi, it's Janelle! Please leave me a message. And have a groovy day!" Then, a *beep*.

Graham hung up and called again.

"Graham, look!" cried Addy. She jabbed her finger at the windshield.

Graham looked, but didn't see anything.

"In the snow!" said Addy, still pointing.

Then Graham spotted it—a little rectangle of pale blue electronic light partially covered in the snow on the pavement out in front of the SUV. The light came on, went off, then came on again.

It was their mother's phone.

Graham gasped in terror. His mother must have dropped her phone when the night-beast grabbed her.

Addy and Graham traded a look, but before they could do anything else, the SUV lurched heavily, and a shadow passed over the snow-covered window. They heard sounds. Then the SUV shook and lurched again. The beast was out there in the snow, lifting one side of the SUV, trying to flip it over the guardrail.

That's when Graham realized that there are many wild and unknown regions in the world, and no one knows for sure what creatures and dangers lurk in the dark mountains of winter.

The interior light of the SUV came on, and the tailgate swung open.

Graham and Addy spun around to look, and there stood their mother and Bryan in the driving snow.

"Mom! Bryan!" cried Graham, his eyes wide. "You're *alive*!"

"Very funny, Graham," laughed his mother. "Yeah, we're alive. But we're soaking wet. We have a flat tire."

"Here," said Bryan. "Take these." He gathered up the black garbage bags full of Christmas presents that were in the rear compartment of the SUV. He passed them up to Graham and Addy. "I gotta get the spare tire out."

"But don't you peek!" Janelle warned again. Then she searched among her coat pockets. "Graham," she said, "could you hand me my cell phone? I must have left it up front."

"No," said Graham. "You dropped it in the snow out there." He pointed.

"How'd you know that?" she said.

"It's a long story," said Addy.

Janelle went to get her phone. In the white blaze of the headlights, the kids saw her making a phone call. Bryan dug around in the back of the SUV. He opened a panel and lifted out the spare tire. Soon a trooper from the highway patrol drove up behind them. Janelle had called for help. The trooper parked her cruiser behind the SUV and turned on her flashing lights for added safety. Bryan changed the tire and soon the family was on their way again.

Back at home, Graham and Addy and Bryan were eager to tell their father, Russ, all about their wild adventure. He had stayed home that Saturday to set up the Christmas lights on their house. Sure enough, strings of lights on the roof and around the windows were twinkling merrily through the stormy darkness when the SUV pulled up.

"Dad!" cried Graham as they burst through the door, "we were attacked by a night-beast in the canyon! It had fangs and claws and a big giant red eye!"

Of course Janelle had already called him to tell

A.M. LUZZADER

him about the flat tire, but Russ listened with interest.

"It's true," said Janelle, laughing. "If by 'night-beast' he means 'moose'."

"You were attacked by a *moose*?" said Russ.

"No," said Bryan. "But we almost hit one. It was a close call. We could tell by its tracks in the snow."

"We spun around in a circle!" Addy added.

Russ raised his eyebrows at this news.

"That's true, too," said Janelle. "We spun around and the tire blew out, but Bryan put on the spare. Bryan and I are freezing cold but I think everyone's okay."

"Sounds like a really rough night," said Russ. "I'm glad you're all safe."

"Mom dropped her cell phone in the snow!" cried Addy.

"Yeah, and she disappeared!" cried Graham.

"Why don't you follow me into the kitchen," said Russ. "I'll make you all some hot apple cider, and you can tell me the rest of the story."

CHAPTER 7
IN THE FOREST OF THE SPIDER QUEEN

Every summer, Milo Crenshaw stayed with his Grandpa Stu in Arizona. Milo loved Arizona—for the most part, anyway. There was one thing Milo *hated* about Arizona, something terrifying.

But we'll discuss that later.

For now, let's focus on the things Milo *loved* about Arizona. First, Milo's Grandpa Stu lived there. A retired forest ranger, Grandpa Stu stood tall and thin, with a head of wild hair and a bushy beard of silver hair that reminded Milo of steel wire. Grandpa Stu could hike for miles and then chop a mountain of firewood, but he was also kindhearted and easygoing. Grandpa Stu had lots of interesting stories, too, and he seemed to know everything. If Milo ever had a question, Grandpa Stu always had a good answer.

The next reason Milo loved Arizona was that Grandpa Stu lived on the banks of Lake Araña, a vast reservoir deep in the desert. During the school year, Milo lived with his mother in a big city on the other side of the country. It was a nice place, but Milo loved getting away from the busy streets and constant noise to swim in the quiet lake and fish from his grandfather's motorboat.

Please don't think less of Milo when I tell you that the final reason Milo liked visiting Arizona was the way his Grandpa Stu treated him like royalty.

Milo's mother put it a different way. "Grandpa Stu spoils you rotten," she said with a chuckle. "He buys you comic books, takes you bowling and camping, and lets you stay up late watching monster movies."

This was all true. In Arizona, Stu had no school, no paper route, and no worries. Milo would have loved his Grandpa Stu no matter what, but other than requiring Milo to make his own bed and help with the housework, Grandpa Stu let Milo do as he pleased all summer long.

Milo arrived one summer at his grandfather's house on Lake Araña. He was very pleased to see his grandfather again, but he'd had a long day of airplane travel to get there, and he fell asleep in the truck as his grandpa drove home. The next morning, when Milo awoke in the bed in his grandfather's guest room, he could only barely remember how he'd gotten there. Arizona was in a different time zone, and it was already dreadfully warm as Grandpa Stu made breakfast. And so when Grandpa Stu asked him what he wanted to do first, Milo said, "Maybe I'll just lie in the hammock and read comic books."

"I thought so," replied Grandpa Stu.

In Grandpa Stu's back yard, there were two small palm trees that stood a little distance apart. Grandpa Stu had a large hammock that could hang between the palms. Swinging in the hammock in the shade with a glass of ice-cold lemonade was one of Milo's favorite ways to start the summer.

Grandpa Stu stood up from the table and said, "You eat your pancakes while I string up the hammock. But you'll have to bring it inside when you're finished. Remember why?"

Milo blinked sleepily. His mind was foggy and his face ran with sweat. Yes, thought Milo, there was a *very* good reason that Grandpa Stu's hammock must be brought inside—but he couldn't remember it at that instant.

Grandpa Stu reminded Milo with one word: "Spiders."

Milo's eyes snapped open. Of course. If you left the hammock outside, the spiders would take it over. The hammock was made from some kind of coarsely woven woolly rope, and spiders seemed to love it. Milo remembered that he'd once left the hammock out for just one night, and in the morning it was infested with spiders of all sorts. It was truly like something out of a monster movie.

Oh, and this might be the right time to mention what it was that Milo *hated* about Arizona.

You guessed it: spiders.

Milo was slightly terrified of spiders. At home, this wasn't a problem, because the big city apparently wasn't a great spider habitat. If a spider ever did get into their apartment, it was usually small, and Milo or his mother squashed it with a broom (they took turns).

But in Arizona there were lots of spiders. It often seemed that there were as many spiders *inside* Grandpa Stu's house as *outside*. This included wolf spiders, black widows, and a variety of tarantulas, which (in case you don't know) are disturbingly large—some as big as your hand, and their great curved fangs can deliver painful, venomous bites.

Milo did not mind the awful summer heat nor

the confusing time change. Even the Arizona rattlesnakes seemed to keep their distance.

Spiders were Milo's only objection to staying in Arizona.

This is not to say that spiders in Arizona were a *major* problem. Milo rarely had to deal with them at all. If he saw a spider outside, he avoided it. If he spotted one in the house, in the bathtub or on a window sill, he simply told Grandpa Stu, who knew very well Milo was fearful of spiders.

But Grandpa Stu never squashed them. Instead, he gently captured them with a tissue or an old shoe-box, then released them outside.

"Spiders have a job to do," Grandpa Stu explained. "They eat flies and mosquitoes and dust mites. There's no need to kill spiders."

"But if you take them outside," said Milo, "they'll just crawl right back in again."

Grandpa Stu only smiled and shrugged at this.

And so, after breakfast, Milo went out and lay in the hammock, sipping cold lemonade and flipping the pages of a comic book. This was Milo's favorite part of summer vacation—the quiet beginning, when it was all ahead of him. Soon there would be sunny days at the lake and cool nights at the local drive-in movie theater.

Milo grew sleepy as he daydreamed. His eyes closed and the comic book slouched onto his face. This made him flinch, and he nearly spilled his lemonade. As he blinked himself awake, he saw something advancing down the trunk of the palm tree.

A tarantula.

Goosebumps spread across Milo's skin. The hairs on his neck and arms stood up. He recoiled, barely noticing when the glass fell from his hand and thudded on the sandy ground.

This tarantula wasn't large. It was smaller than Milo's palm, but to Milo it seemed gigantic—the size of a personal pizza. It bristled with brown fur and crept down the tree trunk on long, thick legs. Clustered above its two black fangs were eight unblinking eyes gleaming in the sun like tiny black beads.

Milo's throat constricted and his lips drew back from his teeth, enraged that such a disgusting creature would dare to disturb his relaxation.

This tarantula was not moving toward Milo or the hammock on purpose. If Milo's head had not been clouded with fear, he would have realized that the spider had spent the night hunting lizards in the palm tree and was now simply retreating to its burrow in the ground. It probably didn't even notice

Milo. But Milo's head *was* clouded with fear. He rolled his comic book into a club and made ready to attack.

Then he remembered what his grandfather told him: "There's no need to kill spiders."

Sadly, this did not stop Milo. This bloated beastie would receive no mercy from him. He eased forward in the hammock and gave the tarantula a savage swat with the comic book. There came a sickening but somehow satisfying *crunch,* and the tarantula plopped onto its back in the sand.

Milo peeked over the edge of the hammock. There, not far from the spilled lemonade, the spider lay on its back. The bristling legs groped and twitched for a few seconds, and then the spider was still. Only then did Milo realize that the spider had meant him no harm. He wondered what Grandpa Stu might say about this and felt suddenly ashamed.

He hopped down from the hammock. Then, unrolling the comic book and using it like a spatula, Milo scooped up the tarantula's limp and shattered remains. Beneath the spider, a little puddle of wretched goo collected. Holding the comic book with an outstretched arm and his face turned away, Milo resembled a deranged waiter serving up a radioactive meal. He hurried to the trashcan and dumped the spider along with the fouled comic book.

That evening, Milo and his Grandpa Stu went to the drive-in movie theater. They sat in camp chairs in the back of Grandpa Stu's pick-up truck, watching a summer blockbuster about a superhero who possessed all the powers of a spider. Milo had been looking forward to seeing the movie, but he didn't enjoy it. Instead, he imagined spiders scuttling around his feet. He brushed them away and kicked at them, even though they weren't really there.

"You all right?" asked Grandpa Stu through a mouthful of popcorn. "You seem kinda jittery."

"Hmm?" replied Milo. "Oh, I'm okay. It's this movie—it's really exciting!"

When Milo fell asleep that night, he dreamed of spiders.

In this dream, Milo found himself in a dark, tangled forest, where thousands of black widows, brown recluses, and tarantulas swarmed at him in waves. Milo swatted them away with a giant comic book rolled up to the size of a baseball bat. Smashed-up spiders and disconnected spider legs were flung into the air. Milo's hands and clothes and face were spattered with vile spider goo. Worst of all, Milo thought he saw some hulking monster moving up darkly from behind the hoard of smaller spiders—a queen spider the size of a truck.

Milo woke up.

"Milo, Milo," Grandpa Stu was saying. He shook Milo's shoulder. "Wake up. It's just a bad dream."

Milo gasped and sat upright. His hair and pajamas were wet with sweat. He glanced around for the filthy spider army but in the dim light he saw only the familiar furnishings of the guest bedroom—dresser, nightstand, lamp.

"You all right?" his grandfather asked.

"Yeah, I think so," Milo panted.

"What was your nightmare about?"

"I—I don't remember," said Milo. This wasn't really true, but Milo simply could not talk about it.

"Well," said Grandpa Stu, "better get some sleep. We're going camping tomorrow."

Milo nodded and lay back in the bed, but he slept restlessly.

In the morning, Milo heard his grandfather calling. "Come to breakfast, Milo! I made pecan waffles!"

This was Milo's favorite summertime breakfast, and the thought of the summer's first camping trip somewhat energized Milo. He soon forgot the backyard tarantula and the nightmare of the spiders. He and Grandpa Stu went down to the dock, packed the boat with camping gear and supplies, and set off across the lake to a place they called "Pirates' Cove."

Pirates' Cove may have been the finest place to camp in the entire world. There were lots of trees for shade, a big fire pit for big campfires, and the fishing there was always great. The morning air was cool as Grandpa Stu's motorboat sped across the smooth water.

As they neared the far side of the lake, Grandpa Stu pointed. "Arr, me matey," he croaked in his best pirate voice. "Thar be Pirates' Cove!"

"Land ho!" cried Milo.

Grandpa Stu cut the engine and the boat glided into shore.

"Let's unpack," said Grandpa Stu, "then we'll take a boat ride around the lake."

That is what they did. In the afternoon it grew blazing hot, so they went swimming to cool off. Then they ate sandwiches and drank cold sodas on the boat. As afternoon turned to evening, they returned to camp. That's when Milo realized how very tired he was. He hadn't slept much the night before, and setting up camp and swimming had left him exhausted.

Grandpa Stu built a big fire, and for dinner they

cooked the fish they caught, but the sun was still shining when Milo began nodding off in his camp chair.

"You're tuckered out, little buddy," Grandpa Stu observed. "Maybe we should call it a night."

Milo nodded.

"You hit the sack," said Grandpa Stu. "I'll put out the fire."

Milo nodded again, stood up, and staggered away, but he soon realized he was headed for the lake. He spun around and shuffled off in another direction, but then he blundered into a tangle of sagebrush. After several minutes, and with some walking directions from Grandpa Stu, Milo finally located his tent, burrowed into his sleeping bag, and fell into a dreamless sleep.

When Milo awoke, it was dark. His bladder ached. He had to go. Milo kicked his sleeping bag off and groped around for his boots. He put them on in the dark, and then tried to find his headlamp, but his bladder sent him urgent messages to *go, go, go!* so Milo clawed his way out of the tent and into the darkness.

Standing there in the stillness of the night, Milo felt suddenly that he was not alone. Grandpa Stu was there, of course, snoring quietly in his own tent, but Milo felt another presence. Something that wasn't *human*.

"Just your imagination," Milo told himself, shaking his head. "Forget it."

Grandpa Stu always told Milo to walk fifty steps away from camp before taking care of his toilet needs, so Milo stumbled into the trees, counting his footsteps until he reached fifty. He did his business, fastened up his trousers, and then headed back toward the lake.

But his tent was gone.

And so was Grandpa Stu's tent.

And so was the whole entire camp.

There were no chairs, no fire pit, nothing.

Milo quickly realized he'd gotten slightly lost again, so he turned and went in a different direction.

Again he couldn't find the camp, and now he couldn't even find the *lake*.

Milo walked one way and then another. He could no longer hear the lake and the water shushing on the sandy shore, and the camp was simply nowhere to be found. He wandered some more and became even more lost. Soon he was surrounded by trees and dense brush.

"Grandpa?" called Milo. He was embarrassed to have gotten lost while relieving himself, and so at first he kept his voice low. Then panic rose in his chest, and he shouted. "Grandpa Stu!"

Grandpa Stu didn't answer.

If only he had his headlamp. Then he remembered the small metal case in his pocket. It was about the size of a bar of soap, an old tin box that once held mint candies. Now it contained a few matches and other survival supplies, like string and fishing hooks. His grandfather had made it for him to use if he ever got lost.

"Well," Milo thought, "I'm lost," so he opened the case and felt inside. His fingers found the little bundle of wooden matches. He took one out and scraped it on a rock. The match flared to life but gave off a feeble light, and it stayed lit for only a few seconds. Milo dropped it and lit another, but he knew he'd never find his way back to camp that way, and now there were only four matches left.

Then Milo spotted a light through the trees. He walked in that direction, and the light grew stronger. He pressed on through the thick underbrush. The light glowed from somewhere beyond. It was an odd, greenish light.

"But surely that must be the camp," Milo thought.

He tried to go on, but he tripped on the rocky

ground, bumped his knee on a fallen tree, and something thorny scratched his face. Milo knew he'd break an ankle or maybe even his neck if he tried to continue without a light source, so he shouted, "Hello?"

But his voice seemed to lose itself among the trees.

All at once, an idea occurred to him, and he dropped to his knees. By feeling around on the ground in the dark, he gathered enough sagebrush and dry willow twigs to form a crude torch. Crouching in the darkness, Milo lashed the twigs together with some string from his survival case. Next, he removed another match and struck it.

It fizzled out before the torch was lit.

He tried again. The next match broke in half and then fizzled.

"Only two left," Milo muttered miserably, his hands trembling.

He struck the next match, and with it he set the torch alight, but the sagebrush produced a black, oily smoke that made Milo cough, which blew out the flame.

One match remained. Milo steadied himself and carefully struck it. The match-head sparked and sizzled. Milo waited until it burned steadily, then touched the flame to his torch. He held his breath against the smoke. The torch caught fire and began to glow.

Then, without apparent reason, the flame vanished with a slight *woof*.

Milo was devastated. Night enclosed him, and he again felt that he was not alone. But then he exhaled, and his breath moved across a few smoldering embers. The flame re-appeared, and in another moment the torch blazed brightly.

"Thank goodness," Milo whispered to himself.

Then he stood and looked again toward the eerie green light ahead. It seemed to pulse. It seemed to beckon him. Milo held up his torch and picked his way across the uneven ground.

As he drew nearer to the light, he heard rustling sounds. At first, they came from up ahead of him, but as Milo entered a clearing, the sound was all around him.

Milo stopped.

Something was circling him. No, not something, but lots of little things. Milo lowered the torch to better see the ground. In the flame's flicker, the ground itself seemed to crawl.

The forest floor was alive with spiders.

As in his dream from the night before, there were

brown recluses, black widows, tarantulas, and spiders he didn't know the names of. There were big spiders and small ones, fast spiders and slow ones. They circled him and crawled over his feet and ankles.

Milo's breath came in ragged gasps, and his heart was in his throat. Then he heard something louder. It was the sound of something huge crashing toward him through the woods. Timbers groaned and cracked as it came closer.

The Spider Queen.

Milo could see only her shadow against the night sky, but as she loomed above him, he knew she was not the size of a truck. She was much bigger than that. Milo could do nothing, say nothing. He could only stand there staring at the horrible apparition.

The Spider Queen lowered herself into the clearing. Trees bent and snapped under her weight. She was covered with coarse fur. Her twitching fangs were the size of cargo hooks and sharp as spears. And it was the Spider Queen's *eyes* that gave off the ghastly green glow.

Then, very slowly, the Spider Queen lifted one leg into the air, touched Milo on the breastbone, and pushed him hard to the ground. The torch, already burning low, fell to the ground and was smothered by the seething tide of spiders. Milo lay on his back, the massive hairy foot pinning him to the ground. Next, the Spider Queen lowered her hideous face until her enormous fangs and glowing eyes hovered just a foot above Milo's face. The other spiders squirmed around him, tickling him through his hair and clothing.

Milo knew he was finished. Those fangs surely held enough venom to bring down a woolly mammoth. A single prick would melt him like a candy bar in a toaster oven.

But the Spider Queen did not strike. She held very still, pressing Milo down for what seemed like hours. Eventually, Milo understood.

The Spider Queen *could* destroy Milo, but this did not mean that she *would*. The Spider Queen meant no harm to Milo because Milo could certainly do no harm to the Spider Queen. Milo was harmless to the Spider Queen. As soon as this thought entered Milo's brain, the Spider Queen raised her furry foot, and with a great silent heaving, she backed away into the lightless forest. The Spider Queen vanished from view, and with her the green spider light vanished also.

Milo had time to breathe a heavy sigh of relief,

but then he heard the spider hoard scuttling toward him.

All he could do was run.

Branches and thorns tore at his skin and clothes. Stones skinned his shins and knees. But he could not outrun the spiders. They scurried across his feet and around his ankles, up his trouser legs and over his middle, under his shirt and into his hair. Milo ran, flailing his arms, falling, rising, and running on— until something stopped him in his tracks.

Spider webs.

Milo was trapped in a dense tangle of sticky spider silk. He twisted and kicked, but it was no use. The foul spider hoard teemed over him in dense layers, like blankets. Milo screamed, but the spider hoard poured itself into his open mouth and down his throat.

All at once, something hard and strong took Milo by the arm and yanked him free. Milo kicked and struggled harder. Had the Spider Queen returned? Would she inject Milo with venom at last? Would she suck out his liquefied insides like some huge strawberry shake?

No. It was Grandpa Stu.

Milo held still and blinked his eyes. Grandpa Stu knelt in front of him.

"Milo! Snap out of it! Milo!"

"Wh-where am I?" said Milo. "Where is the Queen? Where are the spiders? And the webs?"

"What?" asked Grandpa Stu. "Spiders? There's no spiders. No. Everything's all right. You must have been sleepwalking!"

Milo was covered in dirt, dry leaves, sand, and twigs. Grandpa Stu brushed them away. Milo noticed the sun was coming up. It was morning.

"Listen," said Grandpa Stu. "What's the matter? Why have you been acting so strange?"

Milo couldn't stay quiet any longer. He told Grandpa Stu about that morning in the hammock, and how he'd clobbered the helpless tarantula.

Grandpa Stu nodded. He was still picking bits of brush from Milo's hair. "I understand," he said. "Is that what your nightmare was about?"

Milo nodded.

"All right," said Grandpa Stu, patting Milo on the shoulder. "You get in your tent and lie down. I'll pack up and we'll head home."

That is what they did.

Back at Grandpa Stu's house, Milo had a bath and ate a grilled-cheese sandwich for lunch. He began to feel better.

"Want me to hang up the hammock?" Grandpa Stu asked.

"No," said Milo. "I think I'll stay inside today."

Grandpa Stu smiled and nodded. "Wanna play some Scrabble?"

"Okay," replied Milo.

Just then, something darted out from beneath the couch. With lightning quickness it scuttled to the middle of the living room and stopped. It was a wolf spider. They're not as large as tarantulas, but they're creepy in their own way because of their amazing speed.

Milo jerked his legs up off the floor and retreated to one corner of the couch.

"Tarnation!" cried Grandpa Stu, standing up. "*Another* dag-nabbed spider! Don't worry. I got it." From his back pocket Grandpa Stu whipped out his handkerchief and slowly approached the spider.

But even the sight of Grandpa Stu picking up the spider sent a blood-freezing chill down Milo's back. He remembered his encounter with the Spider Queen and cringed so far backward on the couch he almost fell off the back of it.

"It's all right, Milo," said Grandpa Stu, gathering the spider into his handkerchief. "It's alright to be afraid of spiders. Just remember—they won't hurt you if you don't hurt them."

Milo wondered if what his grandfather said were true. Milo was still afraid of them, but maybe he could learn to live with them.

Grandpa Stu went out the front door and down the steps. Stu watched from a safe distance as his grandfather crouched in the sandy yard, and the wolf spider scurried off and was lost from view in a patch of prickly pear.

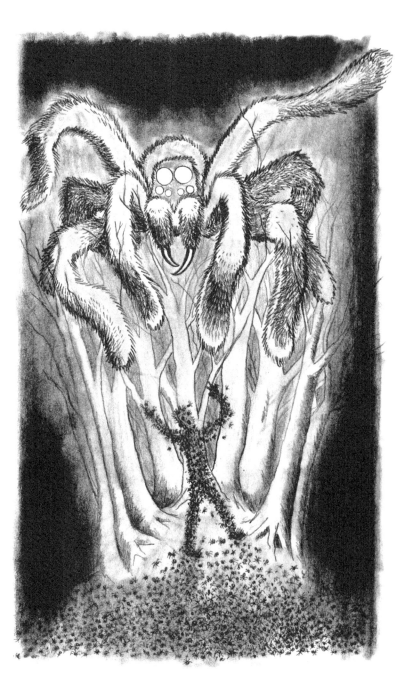

CHAPTER 8
THE DOUBLE-WALKER

Ian Zwilling couldn't wait to get to school.

Not all kids feel that way about school. Some kids can take it or leave it, and others really can't wait to get *away* from school.

But Ian couldn't wait to get there, by which I mean he literally could not wait for school to start at 9:00 a.m.

And so he arrived at 6:58 in the morning.

Ian was twelve years old and rather on the short side. He had curly, light-colored hair and eyeglasses with big round frames. The reason Ian couldn't wait for school to start on that particular Monday was that it was the first day to sign up for the school science fair.

Ian had worked on his science project all

summer, and had cloned a head of cabbage from another head of cabbage by using certain parts of the leaves. Ian's experiment clearly demonstrated the principle that plants can be grown without seeds. Ian wanted nothing more than to win a blue ribbon so that he could compete in the state science fair. If Ian's project got a blue ribbon at the state science fair, he could then compete at the national science fair in Washington, D.C.

This was Ian's fondest hope.

Ian was also keeping an eye out for his good friend Tanner that morning. He and Tanner had been friends since first grade. Ian had told Tanner that he was going to turn in his paperwork early that morning, and Tanner said he might do the same. However, Tanner must have changed his mind, because when Mr. Crickson, the science teacher, arrived at his classroom at 7:42 a.m., he found only Ian waiting for him.

To be clear, Ian could have turned in the paperwork during his science class later that day. He could have waited until after school, too. In fact, it was only Monday, and the actual deadline wasn't until Friday.

And yet there was Ian, waiting patiently for Mr. Crickson.

"I thought I might find you here this morning,"

said Mr. Crickson, smiling and fumbling with his keys to unlock the classroom. "That's your science fair paperwork, I assume?"

"Yep, this is it," said Ian, holding up the papers.

"Wow, that's gotta be twenty pages long," observed Mr. Crickson as he inserted the key to unlock the door.

"Twenty-two and three quarters," replied Ian. "I've included all my findings, data, and several supplemental diagrams and illustrations."

"Well," said Mr. Crickson, swinging the door open, "come on in!"

They went into the classroom. Ian took a seat while Mr. Crickson sat at his desk and read the paperwork.

"This is marvelous!" said Mr. Crickson, reading each page carefully. "The judges are going to love it!"

"All I want is to compete at nationals!" Ian said excitedly.

Mr. Crickson and Ian spoke more, but soon it was 8:41, almost time for the first bell to ring. Ian rose to leave for his first class.

"Well done, Ian!" said Mr. Crickson. "I'll see you in class later today."

As Ian strolled happily to his history class, he

saw his friend Tanner. He was quite tall with red hair. Ian waved and shouted Tanner's name, but the hallway was very noisy and crowded just then, and Tanner didn't seem to see or hear Ian.

Ian was eager to know if Tanner had his science fair paperwork ready, but then he noticed Tanner was speaking to another student, a boy. This boy stood with his back to Ian, and so Ian couldn't see who he was. All Ian knew for sure was that the kid seemed familiar, although this may have been because the kid was about the same height as Ian and he had curly hair, not unlike Ian's own.

But then the bell rang to indicate it was 8:45. Tanner hurried off to class, and the other boy did, too. Ian called out to Tanner again, but he was lost in the crowd. Ian looked around for the other boy, but he'd also disappeared.

Ian shrugged and continued on to history class, and after history he went to biology class. Tanner was in the same biology class, and so Ian took the desk next to him.

"We meet at last," said Ian.

"Ah, hello again, Ian," said Tanner.

Ian nodded and opened his notebook, but then he paused. "What do you mean by 'Hello *again*'?"

"Nothing," said Tanner, shrugging and opening

his own notebook. "Just that we saw one another earlier."

"Oh," said Ian. "I didn't think you saw me this morning in the hallway."

"What a weird thing to say," answered Tanner, furrowing his brow. "How could I *not* see you? You were standing right in front of me."

Ms. Carson, the biology teacher, interrupted. "Settle down, students," she said from the front of the classroom. "Quiet down now."

Ian was confused, but he did as Ms. Carson said.

"Before we start class," she said, "I'd like to remind you that if you're planning to enter the science fair, you must submit your paperwork to Mr. Crickson before next Friday."

Tanner leaned over and whispered to Ian, "It's really too bad we can't go to the science fair together this year."

"What are you talking about?" whispered Ian.

"What are *you* talking about?" replied Tanner.

"I'm talking about my science project!" hissed Ian.

"So am I!" Tanner hissed back.

"*Your* science project?"

"No, *yours*!"

"Ian and Tanner," said Ms. Carson, "please stop

talking. Thank you. Now then, today we'll be discussing DNA. Who can tell me what that stands for?"

For the rest of the class, Ian and Tanner whispered, passed notes, and even employed hand gestures in their attempts to clarify their puzzling conversation, but they were continually shushed by Ms. Carson. The end result was that they became even more confused with one another and even somewhat cross.

When biology class was over, Ian and Tanner stepped into the hallway.

"Okay," said Ian. "What do you mean we can't go to the science fair together?"

"You *withdrew* your project from the science fair!" cried Tanner.

"What are you talking about?" hollered Ian.

"What are *you* talking about?" Tanner hollered back.

And they fell to interrupting one another and shouting. Then the bell rang, meaning they were late for class. Tanner stormed off in one direction while Ian stomped away in another.

Ian shook his head and sighed, still trying to understand what had just happened. He jogged along, hoping he wouldn't be marked as tardy. The hallways were now mostly deserted, but just then Ian spotted a boy approaching him and immediately recognized him as the boy Tanner had been talking to earlier that morning. Ian slowed his pace.

This boy looked familiar.

This boy looked *extremely* familiar.

This boy looked perfectly and exactly like Ian himself.

The other boy had the same hair, same build, and same height as Ian. The other boy even wore the same kind of eyeglasses Ian wore.

The lookalike gave Ian a very brief but somehow *sly* look. Then he passed by Ian without saying a word. Ian, on the other hand, stopped in the hallway and stared in amazement as the lookalike walked on. Ian wanted to say something to the boy, but what? What do you say when you meet *yourself* in the hallway at school on your way to English class?

Excuse me! May I talk to me for a moment?

Ian suddenly realized he was now *very* late for class, and so he continued up the hallway, but he looked over his shoulder as he went.

In English class, the teacher, Mr. McCarthy, lectured about punctuation and paragraphs, but Ian was simply too baffled to listen closely.

Ian's friend Anita sat at the desk behind Ian. She

tapped him on the shoulder and asked, "Are you all right, Ian? You look like you've seen a ghost."

"I think I might have," said Ian, turning to Anita. "Just now I saw a kid who looks *just* like me."

"Ooo," she replied. "You met your doppelgänger?"

"My *what*?" asked Ian. For some reason, his blood turned to ice water at the mention of the strange word.

"Your doppelgänger," Anita repeated, her voice low and slightly spooky.

"What the heck is that?" said Ian with a frown.

"I'll tell you after class," she said.

Ian knew that Anita was interested in legends and mythology, and so after English class, he followed her to the lunchroom. They got in the line.

"So," said Anita, grabbing a tray, "you saw someone who looks just like you?"

"Yes," said Ian. He grabbed a tray, too. "What was the word you said? Bubble-hanger?"

"*Doppelgänger*," said Anita, again with a touch of drama in her voice. "It means *double walker* in German. But are you sure you didn't just see some kid who looks kind of like you? Like Randy Lippman?"

"No!" said Ian. "I know Randy Lippman, and

yeah, he does look a *little* like me, but the kid I saw *was* me!"

"Hm," said Anita, nodding thoughtfully. "That sure sounds like a doppelgänger."

"What's that *mean*?"

"It's a spirit or demon that takes on someone else's appearance. Your evil twin."

When they'd gotten their lunch, they found some seats and sat down.

"Why would a demon take on *my* appearance?" asked Ian.

"Sometimes it's just to make trouble in your life," said Anita, taking a bite of her salad. "Doppelgängers are usually just mischief makers. They do something while looking like you, but then you're the one who gets into trouble."

Ian ran a fretful hand across his face. He hated getting into trouble.

"But other times—" Here Anita paused extra dramatically.

"Other times—what?" demanded Ian.

"Well," said Anita, sipping her chocolate milk, "some doppelgängers want to take over your whole *identity*."

"Like identity theft?" said Ian, his eyes wide. "But that's illegal!"

Anita shook her head. "Identity theft is when some ordinary jerk steals your name, credit card number, and personal information so they can use your money to buy stuff. And yes, it's illegal, but a doppelgänger doesn't just steal your information. The doppelgänger steals *you.*"

It was almost time to go back to class, but Ian hadn't eaten a bite. He was too nervous.

"Thanks, Anita," said Ian. "I gotta go find this—this—double-decker, or whatever you call it."

"*Doppelgänger,*" Anita repeated. "Good luck, Ian. Let me know what happens."

Ian spent the rest of lunchtime wandering the lunchroom and school grounds, but he didn't find the doppelgänger. As he searched the library, however, he heard a voice from behind him.

"Ian! *There* you are!"

Ian turned to see Mr. Crickson coming up behind him.

"Listen Ian," he said, "I was very shocked this morning when you came back to my classroom."

"When I did *what?*" blurted Ian.

"You know," said Mr. Crickson, "you gave me your paperwork early this morning, but then you came right back and said you'd decided you were too busy for the science fair."

Ian's mouth opened and closed repeatedly, but no words came out.

"I wonder if you'd reconsider," said Mr. Crickson. "I think the judges will be very impressed with your cabbage-cloning project. You really could go all the way to nationals."

"Yes!" cried Ian desperately. "I want to be in the science fair!"

"Ah, I was hoping you'd say that," said Mr. Crickson, "so, just give me back your paperwork."

"But I *gave* you my paperwork," cried Ian. "It took me two weeks to finish it! It's twenty-four and three-quarters pages long!"

"Yes," said Mr. Crickson, "but you took it *back* only a few minutes after you left."

"No!" hollered Ian. "That wasn't me! That was my"—he tried to recall the word Anita used—"that was my trouble-maker! I mean my double-maker! My *demon-walker!*"

"Ian!" cried Mr. Crickson with a frown, "are you feeling all right?"

"I gotta go," moaned Ian. "Someone's tryna *steal* me!"

Ian ran crazily around the school and through the hallways. A bell rang to signal the end of lunchtime, and another told Ian he was late for class again. Wandering in a sick, fevered state, Ian somehow found himself standing in a hallway in front of a full-length mirror. He looked into the mirror and straightened his posture. His reflection, obviously, straightened up, too. Ian stuck out his tongue, and the reflection stuck out its tongue. Ian adjusted his eye glasses, and so did his reflection. Then Ian held up his right hand and waved.

But when the reflection waved back, it held up *its* right hand, too.

Now, if you'll think about that for a moment, you'll understand why Ian gasped in horror. When you look into a mirror and wave your *right* hand, your reflection should wave its *left* hand.

(You can try this, if you have a mirror handy. I'll wait.)

It was not a mirror at all, Ian realized, but a doorway. And it was not Ian's reflection, but his doppelgänger.

"You!" Ian shrieked, pointing. "You are not me! *I* am me!"

The double slouched. His face turned suddenly sad and very fearful. Ian thought the look-alike might begin to cry.

"I'm sorry!" said the double, covering his face

with his hands. "I'm so sorry! I'm as confused as you are!"

For a moment, Ian felt sorry for the boy, but then he remembered that this imposter had been wandering around school, spoiling his plans.

"Who are you?" growled Ian, "and why do you look exactly like me?"

The double cautiously approached Ian. He really was a remarkable likeness. Same nose, same curly hair, even the same clothes.

But he wasn't *precisely* like Ian.

He was different. There was something about his expression. The double seemed to know something that Ian did not.

"My name is Ian, too," the double said with a sort of helpless shrug. "Ian Zwilling."

"That's impossible," said Ian. "*I'm* Ian Zwilling."

"Yes," the double admitted. "Apparently, we are *both* Ian Zwilling. We look alike. We talk alike. We are the same person. I don't understand it, and I'm really confused and afraid."

Ian narrowed his eyes and said, "Why did you go to Mr. Crickson's class and withdraw my science project this morning?"

The double nodded, held up one finger, and said, "I can explain that."

Ian (the original one) folded his arms and waited.

"I spoke to Tanner this morning before school," said the double. "He's *my* friend, too, you know, and he asked me if I'd given Mr. Crickson my science fair paperwork."

"Which I *did*," said Ian.

"Right," said the double. "But I didn't know anything about any science project, and I certainly didn't want to go to a science fair I knew nothing about, so I went and spoke with Mr. Crickson, and he gave me your paperwork."

"What did you do with it?" demanded Ian. "That paperwork took me two weeks to finish!"

"Don't worry," said the double, placing a hand on Ian's shoulder. "It's here in my backpack."

"Oh, good," breathed Ian, feeling slightly less angry. "But I don't understand," he added. "Where did you *come from*? Where do you *live*?"

A look of terror spread over the double's face. "Well," he stammered, "I-I live at my *house*, at 1024 Twin Pines Avenue, with my parents."

"But that's *my* house," said Ian, "and *my* parents."

Then the double really did cry. He tried to hold back his tears, but he couldn't. "So where is *my* house and parents?" he (the double) sobbed, sniffling and wiping his eyes with his sleeve. "Where do *I* belong? If that's your house, where will I live? I'm so confused! I'm so afraid!"

"Where *does* he belong?" thought Ian. "Where will he go after school? Where will he live?"

The double stood sobbing into his hands.

"Listen," said Ian. "I'm confused, too. Why don't we go to my house—er, *our* house—and we'll try to figure this out."

"You really mean it?" asked the double, sniffling and wiping his tears. "I've made so much trouble for you already."

"Nah, it's okay," said Ian, patting his double gently on the back. "Maybe my mom and dad—I mean *our* mom and dad—will know what to do."

"Thanks, Ian," said Ian's double.

"You're welcome—Ian," said Ian.

When they arrived at home, Ian's dad was out running errands and Ian's mom was still at work.

"Well, this is my room," said Ian, taking off his backpack and coat.

"Yeah, I know," said the double, taking off his own, identical backpack and coat.

"Oh, right," said Ian.

They both laughed and put their coats and backpacks on the bed.

"Here," said the double, unzipping his backpack. "Let me give you these science project papers." He reached into the backpack and returned the precious paperwork.

"Do you want me to tell you about the project?" asked Ian.

"Sure," said the double.

And so Ian explained the project and showed the double his findings and data. The double immediately understood the concepts and complimented Ian on his work.

"Hey," said the double. "You should display the two heads of cabbage side-by-side and ask people if they can tell the difference between the original and the clone!"

"Wow! Great idea!" said Ian.

"Eh," said the double. "You'd have probably thought of it, too, eventually."

Next Ian and the double played some video games. Ian was unsurprised that his double was just as skilled as Ian himself was, which made the games quite exciting.

"You know," said Ian's double, "this is fun."

"I was just thinking the same thing," said Ian with a smile.

In a very short time, Ian had become quite fond

of his double. After all, they thought the same way and liked the same things. As they went to the kitchen for a snack (both had cheese on toast, with orange juice to drink), an idea began to form in Ian's head.

He began to consider the advantages of having a secret twin.

Why not? They could split up their homework, housework, and yardwork. Who hasn't wished for a clone of themselves? Double-Ian had already given Ian some great ideas about his—*their*—science project. Sure, they'd have to figure out a system to hide the secret, but wouldn't it be worth it? It would be the greatest science project of all!

Just then, at the exact same moment, Ian and his double turned to one another and together said:

"*Why can't we* both *be Ian Zwilling?*"

They laughed about this for a long time, and they would have discussed a plan in more detail, but they immediately realized that their ideas were so similar, they almost didn't have to say a word. All they did was discuss the many benefits.

"One of us could go to the movies while the other does homework," said Ian.

"One of us could sleep in while the other does weekend chores," said the other Ian.

They had numerous similar notions.

And so it was decided. Ian and the double would become one identity in two bodies.

They agreed it would be best for double-Ian to show himself when their parents arrived. This would be the test. Original-Ian would stay in his bedroom while double-Ian had dinner with his parents and did his homework at the kitchen table. If their parents were fooled, they would put the full plan into action.

Ian hid himself in the closet for the evening, supplied with a bottle of water, candy bar, flashlight, and some comic books, and there he waited.

After a while, he heard his dad arrive, and then his mom. Their voices were muffled.

Ian's mom said something like, "How was school, sweetie?"

Double-Ian said, "Oh, fine," or something like that, just as Ian would have.

His dad asked, "Did you turn in the paperwork for your science project?"

And double-Ian said, "No, I had some new ideas to write down. I'll turn it in tomorrow."

"Sounds good," said Ian's dad.

The plan was working.

Ian chuckled a little as he relaxed and read a

comic book. Ian's double and his parents talked and laughed all through dinner.

Then there came a knock at the closet door.

Ian almost jumped out of his skin, but he heard his double's voice.

"It's me," whispered double-Ian. "Open up."

Ian pushed the closet door open a little and saw his double.

"How's it going?" asked Ian, his voice low.

"They don't suspect a thing!" whispered double-Ian. "I think we should move on to phase two."

"Phase two?" asked Ian. "What's that?"

"Stay right here and I'll show you," said double-Ian.

Ian carefully closed the closet door and listened as double-Ian began to scream murderously.

"Mom!" he shrieked. "Dad! Help me! Come quick!"

"What's wrong?" called Ian's mother.

"What's going on?" said Ian's father.

Ian heard them both come running down the hall.

"In th-th-there," said the double, his voice shuddering. "There's someone in my closet! He said he was gonna *kill me!*"

The closet flew open, and original-Ian squinted

up at his father, who jumped back as if he'd seen a rattlesnake. Ian's mother startled back, too. Double-Ian cowered somewhere behind them.

"Who are you?" Ian's father demanded. "What are you doing in that closet?"

He pulled Ian from the closet and dragged him into the living room. Before Ian could say anything that made sense, his father was making a call on his phone.

"But *I'm* Ian! I am Ian!" Ian wailed.

Ian's mother hurried the double away to protect him from Ian. On the double's face, Ian saw the same sly smile he'd seen in the hallway at school that day. He really *did* know something that Ian did not. Ian's father chased Ian around the house, but Ian ducked under the kitchen table, knocked over chairs and potted plants, and ripped pictures from the wall. Soon the red and blue lights of a police car were flashing outside.

Ian's father spoke to the police officers while Ian crouched beneath the dining room table. In another few minutes a doctor arrived.

"I'm not sure what's going on," said Ian's father, gesturing to Ian. "This little boy somehow snuck into our house and hid in a closet. He threatened my son.

He's even dressed in my son's clothes. Everyone's really creeped out."

"Nooo!" the original Ian screamed, crouching beneath a side table. "*He's* not me! *I'm* me! I'm the real one and he's the demon-walker!"

"He just keeps ranting like this," said Ian's father, shrugging, "screaming about demons and spirits."

The adults tried to calm original-Ian, but he screamed and scurried around so violently, one of the police officers finally tackled him.

"The weird thing is," said Ian's father, "he looks a little bit like our son, Ian."

"He's a demon!" howled Ian as the officer wrapped his arms around him. "*A double-demon!* But I'm me! Just ask Anita!"

"This little boy is obviously very disturbed," said the doctor with a worried expression on his face. He knelt down to examine Ian.

While the police officer held Ian still, the doctor took a penlight from his jacket and shined it in Ian's eyes. Ian squeezed his eyes closed and thrashed like a fish.

"It's no use," huffed the doctor, returning the penlight to his jacket. "Let's take him to the hospital for observation and then find out who he belongs to."

The police officer lifted original-Ian and carried

him away to his squad car. Ian never stopped struggling.

No one's sure what happened to the original Ian Zwilling. His "real" parents were never identified, obviously, because they were right there at 1024 Twin Pines Avenue with what they thought was their "real" son. We can only wonder how long the real Ian raved about demons before he began to believe what his doctors told him—that he suffered from powerful delusions. After that, we can assume the boy was placed in an orphanage or some other institution. And even if Ian were by some stroke of extraordinary luck adopted by new parents, could he ever fully recover? Won't you agree that poor Ian (or whatever he was called after that) would not only miss his parents terribly but would also be haunted for life by doubles—seeing his own face peering from the windows of passing cars and spotting imposters in supermarket aisles? Would he not dream of doppelgängers forever more?

On the other hand, the boy who remained at 1024 Twin Pines Avenue, the new Ian Zwilling, was perfectly happy. He did well in school, played video games, and hung out with his friends. In fact, you'll be glad to know that Ian's cloned cabbage really did impress the science fair judges—it won a blue ribbon in Washington, D.C., at the national science fair.

One day, toward the end of the school year, as Ian took a seat in English class, he heard a voice behind him.

"Hey, Ian," said Anita. Her tone was friendly but sarcastic. "You never told me what happened with your doppelgänger. I wanted to know. Have you seen him lately?"

Ian turned to face her and with a nervous chuckle said, "Oh, did I mention that to you?"

"Yeah, of course," said Anita, slightly exasperated. "We spent a whole lunch hour talking about it!"

"I guess I forgot," said Ian, his face reddening.

"Well, did you ever find him?"

"Nah," said Ian, turning back around in his seat. "I don't think he ever really existed."

Bonus Content

Sign up for my newsletter to get a free printable poster set of the illustrations from this book (for personal use only).

https://BookHip.com/VCPGVAL

A NOTE FROM THE AUTHOR

THANK you for reading Arthur Blackwood's Scary Stories for Kids who Like Scary Stories: Book 1.

If you have a few moments, it would mean the world to me if you would leave an honest review about the book on the retail site of your choice. Your help in spreading the word is greatly appreciated. Reviews from readers help make a huge difference in assisting new readers in finding books they'll enjoy.

Happy reading!

Love, A.M. Luzzader

P.S. If you'd like to know when my next book is out and also receive occasional updates on bonus offers, freebies, and special deals, please sign up for my newsletter at www.amluzzader.com.

WWW.AMLUZZADER.COM

- blog
- freebies
- newsletter
- contact info

OTHER BOOKS BY
A.M. Luzzader

Arthur Blackwood's Scary Stories
for Kids Who Like Scary Stories

Releasing
2021-
2022

For ages
8-12

A.M. Luzzader is an award-winning children's author who writes chapter books and middle grade books. She specializes in writing books for preteens. A.M.'s fantasy adventure series 'A Mermaid in Middle Grade' is a magical coming of age book series for ages 8-12. She is also the author of the 'Hannah Saves the World' series, which is a children's mystery adventure, also for ages 8-12.

A.M. decided she wanted to write fun stories for

kids when she was still a kid herself. By the time she was in fourth grade, she was already writing short stories. In fifth grade, she bought a typewriter at a garage sale to put her words into print, and in sixth grade she added illustrations. Now that she has decided what she wants to be when she grows up, A.M. writes books for girls and boys full time. She was selected as the Writer of the Year in 2019-2020 by the League of Utah Writers.

A.M. is the mother of an 11-year-old boy and a 14-year-old boy who often inspire her stories. She lives with her husband and children in northern Utah. She is a devout cat person and avid reader.

A.M. Luzzader's books are appropriate for ages 5-12. Her chapter books are intended for kindergarten to third grade, and her middle grade books are for third grade through sixth grade. Find out more about A.M., sign up to receive her newsletter, and get special offers at her website: www.amluzzader.com.

facebook.com/a.m.luzzader

amazon.com/author/amluzzader

Made in the USA
Coppell, TX
04 October 2022

84044550R00089